About th

Sam Joyson-Cardy is twenty-four years old and lives in Nottingham with his family. He fell in love with writing aged eight with short stories. *Breaking Point* is his first novel and he hopes to write many more.

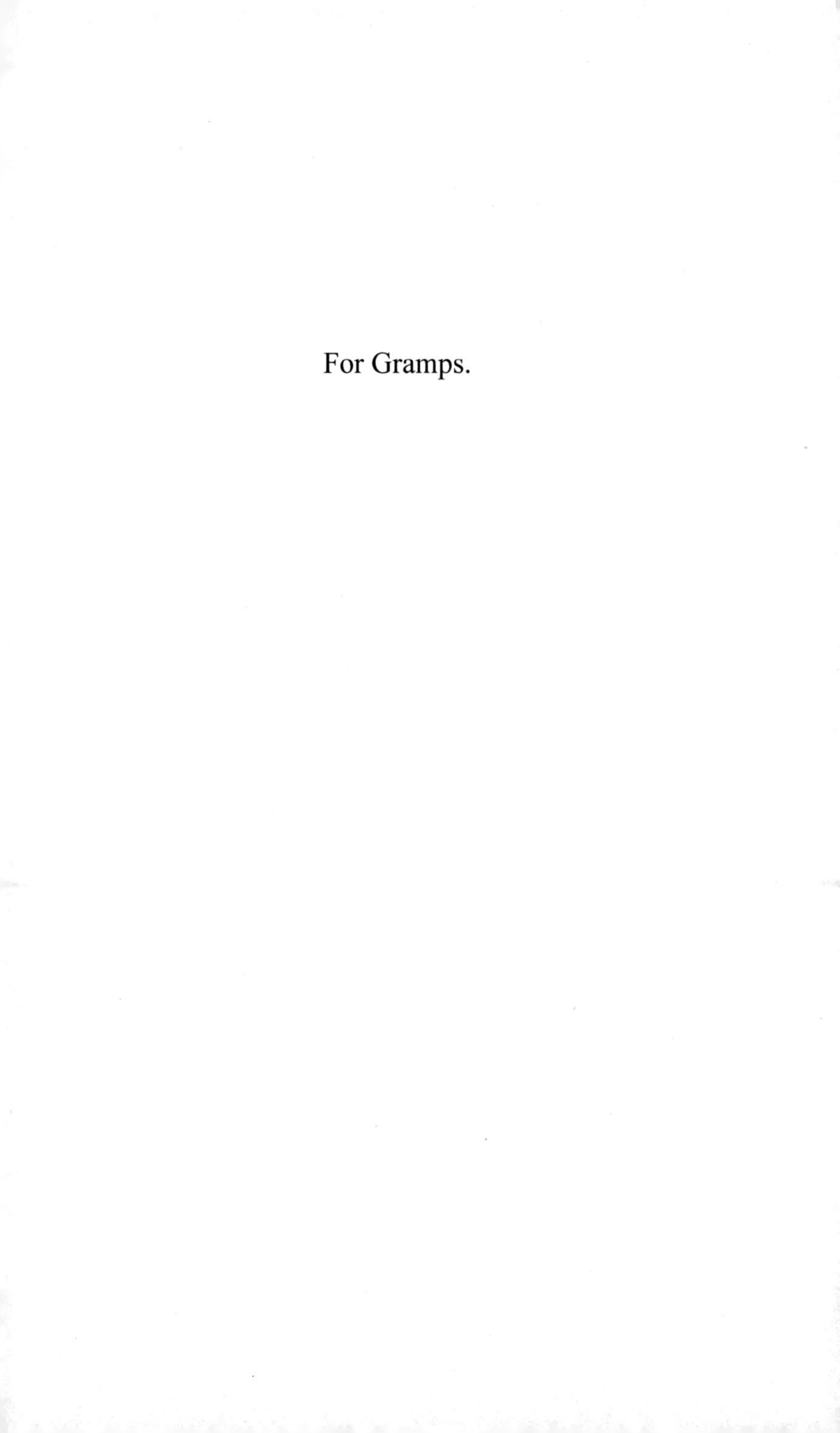

For Gramps.

Sam Joyson-Cardy

Breaking Point

Austin Macauley Publishers™
London • Cambridge • New York • Sharjah

A CIP catalogue record for this title is available from the British Library.

ISBN 9781786290038 (Paperback)
ISBN 9781786290045 (Hardback)
ISBN 9781786290052 (E-Book)
www.austinmacauley.com

First Published (2017)
Austin Macauley Publishers Ltd.
25 Canada Square
Canary Wharf
London
E14 5LQ

Acknowledgements

To Mum, Dad, Josh, Alex, Rhys, Alex K, Alfie, Frank and Eden, thanks for picking me up and kicking me forward when I've needed it.

Chapter One

I don't remember much about the moment I died. The day had been the usual eclectic mix of cigarettes, television and whiskey. The streets had become too dangerous since Bletchley. The Phoenix had shrugged off the charade of innocence. People had begun disappearing from their homes. Self-driving cars had spirited dissidents away, never to be seen again. Home invasions had begun. I was amazed they hadn't caught up with me yet. I had written more of the things the previous months had revealed to me; things I couldn't wait to expand upon, but things that would undoubtedly be hazardous to my health if the book was discovered. I made sure it was hidden away in the second drawer beside my bed; beneath the optimistic condoms, my love life had been in a coma for at least the past five years. Letters I was keeping for their previous importance spread out above them, blanketing the book in dusty foliage of yellowing envelopes. They were so old their importance had probably waned but they served to protect the secrets of the battered old notebook beneath them. I turned off the lights, locked up and lay in bed wide awake, staring at the ceiling. I waited for my mind to stop racing through the thoughts I subdued during the day with drink. The events of the p`ast few months danced above me, haunting me in the shadows. The memories of what had caused them were more painful than any of the scars that had carved themselves into my skin. My eyes closed slowly and I drifted off into a dreamless, restless sleep.

Then it happened. With a sinking sense of inevitability, the silence broke.

The glass shattered with the chilling sound of impending danger. For a moment I just lay there, eyes awake with my sluggish mind taking a few seconds to catch up. My body had already lurched out of bed and was heading for the bedroom door. By the time I had opened the door I was fully awake, adrenaline coursing through my veins. I stepped forwards and swore under my breath, an immediate, sharp pain in my foot had brought me out of the adrenaline fuelled bravado which had me pictured as the suave James Bond type character, disturbing an attacker and kicking the living daylights out of him before returning to bed to a supermodel girlfriend who had been impressed by my macho superhero fighting skills and couldn't wait to show her gratitude, in whatever way she saw fit. The warm trickle of blood brought me out of my ill-timed daydream. I peered through the gloom to see a jagged, clear, piece of glass sticking out of the sole of my foot. It had been stained crimson by my blood. I removed it quickly and limped forwards into the murky midnight darkness of my living room.

The shadowy figure was standing in the centre, the feeble trickle of the street light outside betrayed his outline. He was tall, muscular and searching for something. I watched him for a few seconds pulling books off the shelf, looking through each one briefly before throwing them over his shoulder and continuing on to the next. I had played out this scene in my head many times, the intruder, the James Bond hero mind set; every time it starts with a clear, confident signal of intent, putting the intruder on the back foot, and giving me the advantage to attack in the momentary lapse of concentration brought on by being startled in the middle of something. Instead of a calm clearing of my throat, what actually escaped my body was a strangled warble, shrill, undignified, not in the least bit scary. He turned slowly, he was in control of this situation and he knew it. He was certainly not on the back foot. We circled each other in the gloom. He had already sized me up, I was sure of it. This whole rigmarole was just ramping up the tension, making me feel uneasy in my own home, shifting the balance of power squarely to him. It was working. I wasn't sure if it was the loss of blood or a hallucination, but out of the inky gloom, two other figures, who up until now had been obscured by the obsidian darkness of the living room, now ambled into view.

The next few moments flew by in a blur of knuckles, blood and broken bones. As I say, I don't really remember the moment I died. The flash of the knife, the searing, burning pain as it twisted in my gut. The dizzying nausea as I fell to the floor all whirled together into a sickening blur. Finally, the warm embrace of my own, ever expanding, bloody pool slowly and inexorably made its way toward the corners of the room. I summoned the last reserves of my strength and raised my head out of the already congealing mess which sprawled lazily out from beneath me. Our eyes met as he crouched down next to me. His, calm blue eyes met my brown, which were clouding over, closing slowly. He leered over me in the darkness. My strength failed and I relented to the darkness that engulfed me.

I felt someone cradle my head.

Chapter Two

A FEW MONTHS EARLIER

The fire of the whiskey warmed my stomach against the chill of a mid-winter evening. Outside the street lights sputtered into life, throwing grotesque shadows onto the walls and making all the objects around me look ghostly and unfamiliar. My laptop sat precariously perched on the arm of my chair, humming nonchalantly, the ethereal white of the screen flickering in the darkness. The smoke from my cigarette obscured my vision for a second as I exhaled, dancing up from my lips and disappearing into the abyss beyond the screen. I wasn't sure what I was looking for, just another evening browsing aimlessly, suffocating in the fumes of my own idleness.

Just for a second I was sure my screen wavered, revealing another picture beneath, but no sooner had my whiskey-addled mind recognised it, it disappeared again, leaving me both nonplussed and excited – what happened? What changed, and more importantly, why had it changed? The blood pulsed in my ears, my heart raced, the warm whiskey feeling in my stomach dissipated instantaneously, leaving my mind in a whirl; had anyone else seen this? Ninety-five per cent of the developed world spent more than an hour a day online, chances are someone, somewhere must have seen something. Although I hadn't felt so awake in years, with my mind a buzzing hive of activity, the whiskey had taken its toll, my eyelids acted on their own, closing where I sat, bathed in the glow of the intriguing yet simultaneously mundane screen.

When I awoke, the murky darkness of night had faded to the blood red haze of dawn, caressing the entire room in a comforting glow which seeped into every corner, illuminating all the meaningless trinkets that had cast unfamiliar shadows last night, making them instantly recognisable once again. My skin responded to the warmth of the winter sun's first rays before my eyes finally wrenched themselves reluctantly open. A sickening dread filled the vacant space in my stomach previously occupied by the whiskey. My head pounded, partially due to the aching need for the first cigarette of the day, partially down to the questions that filled my fuzzy mind. Had last night really happened? If it had, what did it mean? How could I find out for certain? I wiped the last remnants of sleep out of my eyes and groaned as I heaved my body into life. As my eyes focused I became acutely aware that I was being watched.

I lived alone.

My momentary confusion was replaced by shock as the adrenaline flooded into my system, I sat bolt upright and stared into the piercingly blue eyes which leered out of the screen at me. The eyes lingered for a few seconds longer then, almost as though the owner of them realised they were being watched, darted furtively from one side to the other then faded into the darkness, leaving me alone and shaken. I'd only slept for four hours; it had taken its toll. I stood up slowly, stretched, groaned and shuffled towards the bathroom. The face that greeted me in the mirror was one that I hardly recognised, the eyes were darkened by lack of sleep, cheeks were sunken and thin, the stubble that framed it clung there as if it was shading them in, aged and greying beyond my 30 years. The steam rose up from the basin. I bent down and buried my face in the cleansing, soothing water.

Fifteen minutes later the eyes on my screen were at the back of my mind, as I stepped out of my front door into the bright chill of a winter's day. I trudged moodily through the snow which had fallen three days ago, it was no longer bright, crisp and fresh, it had begun to melt, greying and freezing again into treacherous ice. All of a sudden, I felt a pair of eyes burrowing into the back of my skull, fixed onto my slouched, moody figure. I turned slowly; glanced over my shoulder as swiftly as possible. The man froze, his long black coat swirling in the icy breeze; he was too far back for me to make out any of his features, but he was tall, slender and watching me intently. I turned completely, to face him, to confirm that he was actually there. By the time I had turned he'd disappeared, leaving me back in the whirling confusion of the previous night.

I picked up my pace, my heartbeat thundered in my ears, the breath escaped my chest even before I realised it, numbing my hands and blurring my vision. I had to stop, the hyperventilation had come out of nowhere, suddenly, everything became too real, the sheer panic washed over me, paralysing, nauseating, a lump in my throat rose from my chest and lingered, stubbornly refusing to clear, no matter how many times I coughed. I stumbled forwards, my legs weakened, feet splayed on the ice and I plunged forwards towards the pavement.

I don't remember hitting the ground.

The pain in my head rudely woke me up, I could already feel the lump pushing its way out of my skull, erupting outwards, competing with my skin for space on my face. I couldn't see it, but I had a sneaking suspicion that it wasn't the best I'd ever looked. I pushed up from the ground in one sweeping motion, and instantly regretted it. I knew I'd got up too fast. The double vision swayed sickeningly in front of me. Fumbling for my phone I tentatively took my first steps. I found the number I wanted and pressed dial.

The dial tone hummed twice.

"Hey man, what's up?"

The relief flooded through me. "Hey man, are you free, want to get a drink?"

"Sure man, bar, 10 minutes?" came the reply.

"Sounds good, see you then." The phone clicked off, the seconds of silence that followed gave me time to adjust to the blurred vision, which cleared. I shrugged off the snow from my shoulders and trudged forwards towards my favourite bar in the town.

Chapter Three

Joe was already there when I arrived. He spotted me in the doorway and began to stand to attract my attention, before spying Mount Vesuvius protruding out of my forehead, frowning and settling back in his chair. The pint of lager was on the table in front of me, the glass felt cold but reassuring in my hands. Joe took a deep drink from his pint, stifled a belch and looked up.

"What the hell happened there?" He asked, nodding toward my forehead.

"Gravity man, gravity, can't fight it, it will win." I replied slowly, smirking from above the brim of my pint.

He chuckled under his breath and nodded grimly, watching my movements as I tapped nervously on the table, looking around at the other drinkers all engrossed in their conversations, laughing, blissfully living in a communal ignorance that, up until last night, I had shared in. Now, that feeling of wonderful complacency was the furthest thing from my mind. I mused on this, mindlessly scratching at the back of my left hand. My musings were interrupted by Joe grabbing my hand and pulling it toward him.

"Woah, hold up there fella, at least buy me a drink first! We're friends but that's it!" I smirked.

“Fuck you wise-ass,” he scowled, “what the hell is this?”

I gazed down curiously at the hand I’d been scratching. Beneath the skin there was a thin square, about an inch across, barely a millimetre tall, glowing ominously green under the taut pale skin. I pushed it from side to side, there was no give in it at all, whatever it was; it was fixed in there, clinging to the bones with a parasitic tenacity. I sighed deeply, shrugged and looked up. I took a long draught from my pint, set it down fastidiously on the coaster, took another deep breath, and began to relay all the previous twenty-four hours’ events to Joe. When I finished, I looked up directly at the furrowed brow of my best friend, whose eyes remained fixed on the table, fingers running along the carved names of previous patrons who had etched their stories into the eternal fixings of this dingy watering hole.

He paused; his whole body seemed to tighten in the dim lighting around us. His eyes flicked upwards and met my gaze, before hurriedly looking away again. He exhaled slowly, chewed his lower lip nervously as he pondered his next words, like a chess player, studying the board before executing the checkmate move. He tapped the table twice and spoke; his voice barely above a whisper.

“So let me get this straight, you see a pair of eyes coming out of your screen, you’re followed down the street, you pass out, when you wake up you have some sort of Area 51 technology under your skin, and the first thing you think is, ‘I know, I’ll expose my best friend to this risk,’ well thank you very much man, my whole family could be at risk if they know you have associates!” He paused; the fury evident in his emerald eyes. He stood up, looked down at me, shook his head and sullenly stomped out.

I sat there stunned in the wake of his exit. Shit, had I exposed everyone Joe held dear to this? Whatever 'this' was it wasn't good, I knew that much, he had a wife, and a small child, he had a world that he cared about more than anything, and I had stormed in, selfishly bringing him into this chaotic world, which I didn't fully understand myself. As I sat there, mind racing through all the possible consequences of involving my best friend, I happened to glance across the room to see a figure shrouded by the shadowy corner of the bar. As I watched, it stepped out of the shadows, and, even though I was convinced I'd never seen the slender, muscular figure before, the piercingly blue eyes sent an ominous chill through my body. He stood there; the black suit clinging to his muscular frame, a thin, silver tie splitting the darkness of his shirt like a rapier. He was clean shaven, tall, dark hair cut short, functional, flecked with grey. However, if you didn't feel like you'd seen him before somewhere, he could have easily been a bank clerk or lawyer, someone you'd pass in the street without a second thought.

Before I knew what I was doing, I was standing, tentatively taking steps towards the shadowy figure. The bruise on my head throbbed, I suppose it must've always been, but I'd only just started noticing it again. The nauseating pulsation, impossible to ignore, once I had started to feel it again, I wondered how I managed to subdue it for so long. I looked down at my hand, the luminous green was not helping in the slightest, it was the exact shade that could provoke a severe reaction in an instant. The lager began a slow, inexorable journey up my throat, the lump from earlier had returned, then, all at once everything I had eaten and drunk over the past day made a spectacular return. The pain in my skull took over, it was all encompassing, my breathing became shallow, the already dim lighting began to fade, my legs gave out, and for the second time that day, I found myself fading into awkward unconsciousness.

The numbers danced and swum in front of my eyes, I was sure I was unconscious, all the zeroes and ones flashed up and faded, almost on the beat of my heart, almost in a trance I continued to watch, as the numbers continued their hypnotic ballet. Then, out of the darkness, the man from the bar stepped forwards, walking assuredly around inside the very walls of my mind. He stopped, turned to face me and began to speak.

"You don't know me, but I know you." His words reverberated around the interior of my skull, echoing eerily backwards and forwards, almost tangible behind my eyes.

He continued.

"You have seen something that you should never have seen; therefore we have had to take matters into our hands." His deep voice chilled me, what the hell was this? Some kind of fucked up lucid dream, a hallucination, a spiked drink?

"Right now, you're probably thinking this is all some kind of dream, a spiked drink, that I'm just a figment of your imagination, because of that bang on your head? You're wrong. Events have been put in motion which cannot be stopped. We'll meet soon."

Then, just as quickly as the dream had begun, it ended, like someone had flicked a switch, the numbers faded, and the last thing to disappear into the darkest recesses of my mind were his piercing blue eyes, which lingered for just a second too long.

Chapter Four

As they disappeared, I awoke with a start, the sweat pouring off my forehead and running down the back of my neck, I was trembling, the thumping in my head came back almost instantaneously, reminding me I hadn't had a cigarette since last night. I rolled over and reached for the battered pack on the bedside table, I frowned, although it was dark outside, my hand was illuminating the room enough for me to see the royal blue of the cigarette packet reflecting in the glow. I reached inside it, and retrieved the slender, brown tipped stick. I rolled it in my fingers for a moment before putting it to my quivering lips. Swinging my feet over the side of the bed, I cradled my head in my hands, cautiously avoiding the epicentre of the impact from earlier. I took a long drag on my cigarette before looking around my room, squinting in the gloom that seemed to press in from the walls, making my generously proportioned room feel like an airtight coffin. The bookshelves loomed high above my head, the window, which overlooked a field, felt more like a porthole in the hull of a submarine, I pressed my forehead to the glass and felt the cooling sensation spread over the pain in my head and calm me down in tandem with the comforting smoke of the cigarette which snaked up from the tip and curled around my chin, reflected eerily in the green glow of my hand.

My hand.

I had no idea what had happened to it, how the implant, or whatever it was had got there, let alone what it was for. How long had it been under my skin? The chill of terror returned, penetrating my chest like an icy dagger. It occurred to me that my heart was beating at its usual rate, regardless of the feelings swirling around my chest, ticking over like a metronome, relentless, but finite, marching mercilessly towards whatever fate I could see barrelling towards me over the horizon. It was clear now, after my fraught conversation with Joe, that I was on my own, I couldn't involve anyone I cared about, not without exposing them to an inordinate level of danger. Resigned to this fact I sloped into the living room, opened my laptop and sat there, mired in my thoughts. Surely, someone somewhere must know about this, have answers, maybe even have been exactly where I am now. But where to start? I was trying to keep my mind from rushing ahead of me, I needed somewhere to write down the ideas that were tearing through my mind and preventing me from forming a coherent plan. I took another long drag on the cigarette, only to find it had extinguished itself in the time it had taken me to transfer from one room to the other. I re-lit it and inhaled deeply.

The cigarette dwindled to an ashen relic at the edge of the shortened and empty Pringles can which had become my makeshift ash tray as I twirled the pen in my hand. I had figured that the best way to avoid the prying eyes of the organisation, whoever they were, was to keep as much of my writing out of the computerised world as was physically possible. So far I hadn't got as far as I'd hoped with my thoughts, but I had compiled a list of possible organisations that may have had some involvement in this. MI6? CIA? The Army? Al-Qaeda even? Whoever they were, they were sure to have contacts who could instil fear and doubt in the hearts of anyone who may cross them. The second list I'd compiled were reasons they'd come after me. I had a chequered internet history, but no more dubious than any other permanently single shut-in with a Wi-Fi connection, and I'm pretty sure that my extensive knowledge of internet pornography wasn't a reason to attract the attention of a ruthless group who could attach a piece of suspect technology to the hand of someone who, to his knowledge, had never been in trouble with the law, or any gangs for that matter, in his life. You tend to remember that sort of thing.

I suddenly felt a huge surge of frustration, the incessant green glow, the not knowing what it was, all of it became too much. I swept out of my chair, darted into the kitchen and found a knife. There was a faint scar along the far side of the square, presumably where 'they' had inserted whatever it was into my hand. I doused the blade in whiskey to disinfect it, took a generous swig from the bottle for myself, and jammed the knife into my skin. The pain was blinding, almost stunning, and made me stagger back briefly, drawing a sharp breath as the blood spurted out over the back of my hand. In one swift move I pulled the knife along the scar tissue, exposing one edge of the green square. My view was still obscured by the blood and skin that covered the top. I groaned, swore, took another long drink from the bottle and delved back in.

Half an hour later, my home surgery was complete, I looked grimly down at the exposed back of my hand, before examining it closely, I grabbed a tea towel off the side and wiped down the worktop, the blood wasn't absorbed completely, and I ended up just pushing it to a corner to be wiped up later. Grabbing my camera from the other work surface, I returned to my hand, I took a few cursory snaps of the green square, which I could now tell wasn't entirely green. Instead, it was a greyish sliver of metal, with a tiny green screen in the centre. There were some characters scrolling along it, but it was too small for me to make out, especially as the blood loss was beginning to get to me, making my head spin in tandem with the whiskey. I shrugged, sniffed and began to pull at the square. No sooner had I begun to try and free my hand from this alien protrusion, the screen glowed scarlet and began to pulsate. Then without warning, a shock blasted up my arm, throwing me off my feet and across the kitchen.

That hurt. That really hurt.

The numbers made an unwelcome intrusion into my head again in my unconscious state. The figure's deep voice boomed out across the void, although his body didn't appear.

"Nice try. That shows a level of commitment that we were not anticipating," he paused, "our plans shall be accelerated."

Once again the switch was flicked, my eyes opened, and the fear flooded through my veins. I sat up, looked around and realised that I was covered in blood. I cleared up slowly, avoiding using my hand, as it was still raw from the assault of the square. All the while, my mind raced; what plans? How long had they had me in their sights? Most of all, what did they want with me? The clean-up took me another half an hour. When I finished, I made a quick sandwich, retreated to the living room, and wrote up what had transpired in the previous hour. I didn't like the idea of having to put the photos I had taken onto my laptop, but thanks to the inexorable rise of digital photography, and my lack of knowledge when it came to dark rooms, I had no other option but to print them from my computer in order to add them to my book. I grunted, the fact was, if they had been watching me for that long, they would already know it was my only next move.

One thing thundered through my mind like an express train; I was running out of time.

Chapter Five

The knock on the door startled me out of my thoughts; a furtive, short burst of three raps. Clear, sharp, and breaking me out of my slumber. I sat up; three raps once again rang out through the silent hallway of my apartment. I stood up slowly, suspicions buzzing through my mind, every sinew straining against moving towards the door. Since I had decided not to involve anyone close to me in this, then no-one who was behind my front door could be good news for me. My hand moved towards the lock above the handle, clicked it downwards. My arms went numb, the door I'd opened so many times in the four years I'd lived in this flat felt unusually heavy, like the gates to a medieval castle, safe, impenetrable, protective. I peered slowly round the corner, holding my breath. The man in the hall stood there, nervously scanning the corridor for, presumably, anyone who wasn't him or me. He shuffled nervously from one foot to the other, his baggy beige trousers rustling; whoever he was, he wasn't trained in the art of stealth. His long green overcoat was covered in badges, largely along the same theme, "Who shot JFK?" "The truth is out there" "Elvis isn't dead" et cetera.

"Oh brilliant," I groaned, rolling my eyes before opening the door fully, "I'm sorry, I'm not interested in anything you're selling, or turning to Jesus either."

His confused eyes narrowed.

"What? Oh, right, the door knocking," he warbled in hushed tones. "Just let me in ok? We can't talk out here, someone may see!"

I shrugged, he didn't look a threat, and even if he did try something, the James Bond part of my ego convinced me I could take him down. I reluctantly stepped aside to allow him to pass. He took one final cautionary sweep of the corridor and shuffled hastily past me into the hallway. He sloped into the living room and flopped down onto the sofa, the satchel I hadn't noticed before, dropped onto the floor beside his boots. I walked in from the hallway, after ensuring the door was locked again. I lit a cigarette and looked over the glowing orange tip at his jowly face. "So what can I do for you?"

He fumbled in the satchel and retrieved an inhaler and took a deep draw on it. I smirked, asthmatic – of course he was.

He cleared his throat, looked up at me through the haze of cigarette smoke and began.

"I'm so glad I've found you, after all these years! I can't believe I'm here, actually talking to you! They said you weren't coming back, that you were dead, but you're here!" He paused in his fervent speech. "I'm sorry, I don't meant to gush, it's just that I've spent nearly 20 years believing you exist, sacrificed so much, just to be here."

I raised a hand and halted him in his tracks, "What? 20 years? Who are you, why the hell have you been following me, especially since I was 10!"

His brow furrowed, "Since you were what?"

He reached into the bag again and pulled out a battered file, full of photos, dates and newspaper articles on faded, stained paper. He flicked through it, turned it so I could see and pointed. The photo was dated "June 12th 1984". I frowned, the shock coursing through my system.

It wasn't possible.

The eyes that followed me out of the aged pages and stared back into mine were my own. If I really was only 30, then I wasn't even born at the time this photo was taken. The man in the photo stood in a laboratory, his eyes bright with excitement, smiling with a glowing hand, which even in black and white had a distinct off-white hue. I glanced at my hand, the green glow unsettled me now more than it had done this morning. I took a long drag on my cigarette and straightened up. I paced nervously around my front room, my brain buzzing. I turned to face him. "Look," I paused, realising that I didn't actually know his name, I gestured vaguely in his direction.

"Mark."

"Right, look Mark, I don't know who you think I am, or for that matter you are!" the anger swelling in my chest, "you come in here, don't tell me anything useful, and show me a mocked up picture of me a year before I was born!"

He looked visibly shaken by my analysis of the situation; he evidently had a different idea of what his 'revelations' would mean to me. Regaining his composure he stood, looked me straight in the eyes and began to speak, lip quivering.

"You were the greatest scientific mind of a generation, your research was legendary," he took a deep, shuddering breath, "it was magnificent, you were going to change the world, medicine, politics, computing, every possible aspect of life as we know it, changed forever!"

I took a long drag on my cigarette, exhaled slowly and turned away from his unwavering watery blue eyes.

"So," I began, still trying to piece together what Mark was trying to tell me in my head, "this," I nodded at my hand, "was what? Some magic device, meant to heal the sick, give sight to the blind, and make you irresistible to women?" I raised an eyebrow.

He sputtered out a nervous laugh, "Yes, essentially, apart from the irresistibility to women thing, that was the general idea."

I shook my head. "Well, if it wasn't going to make me irresistible to women, really what was the point?" My sarcasm was completely lost on him that time.

"There was only ever one made as far as I know, the one you have in your hand, and as far as I know, the technology was deemed too dangerous after… well…" His voice trailed off nervously as he lowered his gaze to the scrapbook on the table.

I followed his eyes down to the article the book was opened at. It had been highlighted and underlined in various places. It was more tattered and worn than anything I'd seen in the book so far. The confusion and fear only built in my mind when I began to read the headline.

ACCIDENT AT GOVERNMENT LABORATORY KILLS SIXTY.

August 15th 1984.

An accident last night at a secretive government laboratory has claimed around sixty lives according to early reports. A spokesperson for the experimental facility said that a small team of scientists and assistants were working on a highly dangerous project which had gone wrong, reportedly killing all involved.

The following statement hit me like a train. Joe's name preceded the quotation that had been picked out by Mark in luminous green highlighter.

"Naturally this accident has come as a terrible shock to all here, and we will be investigating fully the causes in order to determine what went wrong. Obviously no amount of sympathy can comfort the families of those involved, nevertheless it goes without saying that our thoughts and prayers are with them at this difficult time…"

The sight of Joe's name in connection to any of this had rocked me entirely. Shakily I sat on the edge of my sofa, trembling, hands clenched in front of my face, head bowed.

The article was interrupted by the paper being ripped roughly in order to accommodate the thoughts that Mark had hastily scrawled around the perimeters. I looked up, "What happened that night?"

Mark shrugged. "No-one really knows, the lab was so secure that the records from that night were only available to the top level of investigators, and were destroyed as soon as the investigation was ended."

A disappointment sank my heart from my chest to the pit of my stomach, maybe if I knew what had happened, talk to someone who had been there; maybe this whole crazy ludicrous scenario would make some sense. "What was this project they were working on?" I muttered.

Mark halted and looked down at my hunched frame. "First of all, you should stop saying 'they' and start saying 'I'." He paused, took a deep breath on his inhaler again, shrugged, and continued, "I don't know, in all honesty, it was a top secret project by a privatised company that had to masquerade as a governmental experiment because of the nature of whatever it was."

My mind whirled, incapacitated by what I was hearing. I was involved in something so secret and so dangerous that it had to be called 'classified government business' to keep journalists and pressure groups from prying their beaks into it; and whatever it was, how the hell was Joe mixed up in it? It didn't make sense.

"So…" I prompted.

"So, the only departments that the government were attempting to develop were defence, espionage, and space technologies, so whatever you and your colleagues were working on, was massive, and probably highly dangerous."

I sat down shaking my head; the nerves churning through my intestines, whatever I was doing, wouldn't have been good for the innocent people, the technology would've been used for destruction, why was I even involved? If I had been at all, too many questions, not enough time to even start on figuring out some answers. "How many people actually died that night?" I asked, tentatively.

"The estimated figure was sixty," Mark gestured towards the article, "but someone I spoke to worked on the investigation and they said they had only found fifty-nine bodies in the wreckage."

My heart began to thump in my ears, making it impossible to think straight, could it all be true? Could I have been there? It's not possible, I reassured myself, I wasn't even alive when this accident happened, the chip in my hand, none of it, I got the feeling that Mark was bullshitting me, toying with my mind, with some photos he'd mocked up during his long, lonely nights.

Something to keep him from reality, a fantasy that some had maybe indulged until it became too real for them.

I stood up to face him. “Ok, it’s time to go, this has all been very entertaining, and I’m sure whoever taught you to use photo-shop must be very proud of themselves, but none of this is real, I wasn’t even born when any of this happened, whoever this organisation are, they’re nothing to do with me.”

He stood there, stunned, rocking back and forward on his heels, the anger flickered in his eyes. “So you’re telling me that I somehow conjured all this evidence? Made it all up?”

I nodded, “Yeah, you know for a lunatic you catch on pretty quick.”

His lips curled back into a snarl. “A lunatic? I travelled so far, gave up so much, had to hide where I was from my family and my friends, just so I could come here, and stand in the presence of one of my idols, to be told I’m a lunatic! You know what, fuck it, you’ve had the best years of your life taken from you without even realising it, and I thought I could’ve been the one to save you from them again. For a brilliant mind, you are so… dense, even when the evidence is under your nose, you don’t see it. Do me a favour and stay hidden, with any luck they don’t know you’re here, and you may just get to live to see your ‘thirty-first’.”

With that, he slammed the file shut, shoved it back into the battered old satchel, flung it over his shoulder and stomped to the door. I didn’t follow him. I was left stunned in his wake, the door slammed behind him, causing a shockwave that reverberated through the flat. If there was only one thing Mark had confirmed to me, something I already knew myself, but didn’t want to acknowledge, it was that they, whoever they were, were coming for me.

Chapter Six

My solitary confinement had been ongoing for about three days now, and it was taking its toll. It was a mixture of fear and resentment that kept me glued to my chair; mindlessly channel hopping, in the hope that I'd get some sort of inspiration as to what to do, or where to go to get answers to the sickening soup of questions which made it impossible to plot a route out of this hellish nightmare. The heady mix of whiskey and cigarettes neutralised the fear that bubbled to the surface whenever I began to sober up. I knew that this self-hindrance had to come to an end and soon. The book rested on my lap, with the pen hovering above the pages, poised to be called into action, like an over-eager private awaiting his first orders from a battle-weary commander. Without any warning, and with my eyes completely open, the numbers from before swam in front of my gaze. The pen danced on the paper without me really being in control of it, scrawling out the report it had been so craving for the last hour.

2, 7, 9, 5, 3, 1, 1, 4, 8, 1, 0, 0, 1, 0, 1, 4, 6.

When the numbers faded from view again, I looked down slowly, what the hell did these mean? Why did this happen? Up until now, all of the contact I'd had with this shadowy organisation had come through one figurehead, minimising the risk of me seeing anything that could give me a foothold in the world that I had been thrust into without consent. But now there was this, a golden ticket. A spark of nonsensical hope sprang up from the depths of my belly, rising through me like a phoenix from the ashes of my despair, warming me more than the substantial amount of whiskey I had consumed ever had done. Then, with a crushing realisation it was gone. What had they given me? Some numbers, useless figures that may as well be the telephone number of a pizza place. My stomach contracted and growled, reminding me that I hadn't eaten properly in hours. I phoned the pizza place around the corner from my flat, lit my third, or was it fourth, cigarette, and waited for the doorbell to announce the arrival of my food.

Moments later, and I mean moments, the doorbell rang. My face contorted into a frown. There was no way that could be the pizza delivery, unless, of course, the delivery boy had swapped his under-powered moped for a wormhole, and was delivering pizzas via the space-time continuum. Ignoring the nerves that had begun to swirl around in the pit of my stomach I headed for the door, stopping in the kitchen to conceal a serrated knife up my sleeve. The lack of spy-hole or chain put me on edge immediately; it meant I had to open the door in order to see who was on the other side of it. Sighing heavily, resigned to the idea that whoever was on the other side would not be a bearer of anything good, I opened the door slowly, peering through the gap, when I was confronted by a woman in black. She was average height, athletic, with short dark hair which gently flickered around her chin in the late evening breeze. The draft of cold air blew into my flat, carrying out the fumes of three days in isolation. She recoiled slightly, I couldn't blame her. I'd become used to the pungent mix of congealing metallic blood, Dettol, scotch and cigarettes, which permeated every corner of the flat and clung to everything that occupied it, including me.

"Get in the car." Her voice was soothing, not high, but not masculine either, though what she'd said had done nothing to calm the terror that flowed through my veins, making me incapable of truly appreciating her beauty.

"I would, but I've got pizza coming, and you know what delivery drivers are like if they think you've prank called them, I mean, they know where you live," I retorted gruffly.

"No you haven't, we cancelled it," came her almost instant reply.

I snorted derisively. "I don't know who the hell you people are, putting a chip in my hand and following me is one thing, but fucking with my pizza, that's a bridge too far."

A smile flickered around the corner of her lips for a fraction of a millisecond.

"Come on," she whispered enticingly, "we've got food where we're going."

I shrugged and stepped out of my door, almost without thinking. I glanced into her in near violet eyes, "Bet it's not Giuseppe's though."

She nodded, "I'll make you a deal, you leave the knife here and we'll stop at your pizza place."

I scowled, "Done."

I mean, I needed the knife, but I had my priorities, and besides, if they knew I would take the knife, the chances are they'd have precautions in place to ensure I had literally brought a knife to a gun fight. My suspicions were confirmed as I turned back into my flat.

Glancing out of the corner of my eye, I saw her place her hands on her hips, revealing a black holster and the glinting silver desert eagle nestling within it. I shuddered with a sense of foreboding, what was I doing? I knew not to get into cars with strange women promising pizza, I'd been suckered before. At the same time though, none of those women were carrying high-powered pistols. Which if push came to shove, I'm sure this one wouldn't have any hesitation in using.

Four minutes later, I was sitting in the back of her car, she was next to me, staring out of the darkened window at the pedestrians aimlessly wandering towards bus stops, or clinging to the hands of their lovers as they hurried towards their comfortable abodes in order to escape the winter's icy clutches. A sudden pang of sadness hit me; the touch of a lover's lips against mine was something that I doubted I'd ever feel again.

Giuseppe's was a typical back-alley pizza joint, grimy floors and windows which carried every one of the twelve years of grease, drunken vomit and secret rendezvous between high flying city business men and the hookers, who gave them the things their Stepford wives could only read about during the long, lonely days in suburbia, like a badge of honour. The familiar greasy pizza smell wafted from the narrow doorway, embracing me like an old friend.

Half an hour later; we were back in the car, she, Miss A, I had heard the driver refer to her as, had rolled down the window a millimetre in order to allow some of the vapours from my gigantic hot and spicy to escape the car, without allowing any accidental intrusions from passers-by. I didn't particularly like the heat of the jalapeños, but I figured fuck it, they had pulled me out of my home without warning, cancelled my original pizza order and driven me out to the countryside for reasons which hadn't quite become apparent yet so this was my small rebellion; and Giuseppe made a hot and spicy which clears the nasal passages of anyone within a 10 mile radius along with obliterating the taste buds of the buyer. I couldn't help but chuckle to myself, which brought Miss A out of her musings, she turned to face me, "What?"

I smiled, "Oh nothing, just thinking about when we can look back at this and tell our kids about it as our first date."

The perfect brow creased briefly, obviously the concept of a joke was lost on her, and frankly I felt wasted here. By the time the tension had passed we arrived at the disused scrapyard which became apparent was our destination. I finished the last crumbs of my pizza, stepped out of the car, turned to the guard at the door, handed him the box. "Find a place for that, there's a good chap, Jeeves," I muttered, winking slyly as the expression of dead eyed concentration broke for just a second. It made me feel calmer for a moment, gave me time to collect my thoughts. The nerves had re-surfaced with a vengeance as soon as the bitter night's cold swept in across the desolate junkyard that this murky organisation had decided to make its home.

Chapter Seven

We trudged in silence towards the dingy cabin in the far corner, illuminated only by the torches on the rifles of the guards, and the alien green glow of my hand, which had changed back from the scarlet of impending doom moments before the knock on my door earlier that evening. Miss A reached out towards a panel in the wall, it slid upwards to reveal an indentation of a hand. She leant forwards and pressed her perfectly manicured hand onto the steel plate. What happened next came as a shock, if only to me. Miss A's hand made contact with the plate and, the whole of it glowed a vibrant, fluorescent yellow. I glanced at my own hand, which remained resolutely green. She saw my expression, winked and beckoned me forward. Instinctively I followed, like a lamb to the slaughter. A lamb, however, that had been led there by what could only be described as the closest thing to a goddess the poor, befuddled, and inappropriately aroused lamb had ever seen.

We stepped inside the cabin. It was definitely not what I had been expecting. The room was well lit and airy, with strip lights that hung from the ceiling, framing the crazy scene below like the most ludicrous cartoon fantasy my mind could conjure. Men wandered from one screen to another, furtively pointing and whispering into the ears of white-coated colleagues who sat, transfixed, eyes front, typing manically. All of them, the men standing in black, their scientist buddies, the guards, all had glowing hands, a myriad of colours. What could they signify? Rank, age, profession, squad? I scanned the room, no green ones, none at all. In the corners, giant shimmering cloths covered some kinds of machinery which loomed high above the minions who scurried around; in and out of the coverings which sparked and crackled, making the air thick with a tangible static charge, carrying parts and tools, the like of which I'd never seen before. Hushed whispers followed us through the room, quick stares that dissipated into nothing as we passed; nervous looks over shoulders when the 'drones' thought they weren't being seen. The discomfort stirred in my chest, like a dragon uncoiling after a long slumber. As we marched through the central aisle, a plan began to form, slowly, like the seed of an idea stirring at the base of my skull; a plan began weaving together like the threads of a tapestry. I needed one more piece to complete it though, a piece, I suspected, which would be revealed on the other side of the door we had arrived at whilst I was in my pensive state. The final, elusive piece; where did I fit into all of this?

The door was deadlocked, the same panel as before slid out of the wall, Miss A turned to me, smiled and whispered, "Your turn."

My heartbeat thundered in my ears, drowning out the sounds of the scientists bustling about behind me, almost in one swift movement my green hand swept towards the panel. The moment my fingers began to brush the cold steel, the luminous green began to glow even brighter, highlighting the cuts I'd made days ago, the jagged edges fading into the green light which was spreading down my arm, inside my very bones. The same sequence of numbers flashed up in front of my eyes, for all of a second; then vanished again. Locks clicked sequentially, the door swung back slowly to reveal the interior of the room.

With a chilling realisation I stepped forward. I had been here before, the déjà vu was overwhelming, I hadn't just dreamt that I'd been in this room; I had been in this room. Instinctively, I knew it had two long walkways stretching out parallel above me, with small glass cubicles where more of the white-coated drones tapped away in front of their screens, hands glowing blue whilst their eyes fought a constant battle with the resolute encroachment of their eyelids. Guards paced lazily along the balconies, rifles swinging in front of them. It was probably about four in the morning, judging by the bleak amber glow which was trying to break past the stout inky midnight blue of a winter's morning. It would be changeover soon; a fresh squad of guards would come to relieve their colleagues, who had been on the night shift. How did I know this? I didn't quite know.

The instantly recognisable voice boomed out from above me, I glanced up reluctantly, the memories were beginning to bleed through, vague shadows of a previous incarnation. If I was right, I wouldn't like what I was about to be confronted with.

I was right.

Joe stood there, his creaseless suit unruffled in the air conditioned breeze, his emerald eyes visible from the other side of the room. My heart sank into the chilling fear that had stirred and had begun snaking through my very soul.

"Let me ask you a question," Joe began, smirking through his teeth. He was enjoying this far too much for my liking. "How long have we known each other?"

I paused, brow furrowed. We had known one another a long time, but pinning down a number to the years was eluding me, dancing tantalisingly just out of my reach.

I shrugged, "I dunno, fourteen years?" I glanced up to the balcony; a flicker of disappointment swept his overly composed features, if only for a second. He regained control, staring me down.

He chuckled, "Fourteen years? Fourteen? Do you honestly think we could have built all this in fourteen measly years?" The incredulity in his voice stoked my curiosity, but nowhere near as much as his use of the word "we." Who did he mean? The drones around him, Miss A even? The nagging dread tugged at the back of my mind, some part of me knew what he meant; I just wasn't ready to acknowledge it yet. Just to check, I tested the water,

"I must say, I like the retro vibe you've got going on here," I grinned, nodding up at the panoramic screens that ensconced Joe's vantage point, "very eighties Bond villain. What's next, a shark tank under the floor? Laser cutter aimed at my junk?"

Joe allowed himself a brief chuckle, I'm not sure I liked that, the almost condescension lingering in his glowing, cat like green eyes. "You always were the funny one, but you're mocking your own life's work in this case."

That was all I needed to hear, a sickening punch to the gut. I swallowed the lump that had returned to my throat. A deep shame gently pushed at the back of my head, forcing it down to inspect my shoes. A solitary tear splashed onto the polished surface between my feet, I had no idea what it was doing there, but all the pieces suddenly came together, the green chip in my hand, the follower in the street, all of it, knitting together to illuminate the darkness that had devoured great chunks of my life, still hazy on the details, but making more sense than before.

Joe interrupted my train of thought with a sharp clap of his hands. The shockwave startled me back into the room. He swept down the stairs that curved around and down to the level Miss A and I were standing on. He strolled up to me, unfazed by the "Area 51 shit" that was all around us. His face was so close to mine I could feel his warm breath on my cheek.

"Try thirty-six years." His smile curled around the perfectly straight and perfectly white teeth.

My jaw dropped, the breath caught in my chest. I couldn't help it. Thirty-six years, that was impossible, I was only thirty, and even if I wasn't that would make me nearly fifty! Where the hell had the previous twenty years gone? I mean, I'd had heavy nights before, even heavy weekends, but I could always remember what, and who, had happened the next day. I shook my head.

"That's bullshit – impossible," I sniggered nervously, "I'm thirty years old for fuck's sake!"

"Are you?" he chuckled, eyes narrowing, his voice barely above a whisper, "are you sure?"

His eyes narrowed, he stepped away, humming under his breath, just loud enough to be heard above the dull clatter of fingers on keyboards. Pink Floyd.

As he hummed languidly away from us, a door set back in the wall to my right swung open to reveal a quivering, blindfolded woman, whose shaking silhouette cast a feeble shadow on the back of my mind. I recognised her, in the same way you may recognise an acquaintance in the street if you hadn't seen them in years. I had no idea where I knew her from, or what her part in Joe's insanity was, I figured I'd find out soon enough. She stumbled forwards, followed closely by two menacing guards. The barrelled noses of their suppressed rifles jabbed into her kidneys, forcing her into the centre of the room, halfway between Miss A, myself and Joe.

Joe gave a quick nod to one of the guards, who stepped forward, pulled the blindfold roughly from the woman's eyes and retreated to his previous position.

Her eyes skirted nervously around the room, her trembling frame froze when she saw me, the deep, shuddering breath caught in her throat, making her chest heave with the shock and surprise that seeing me had obviously caused her. She blinked with disbelief, looked up at Joe, and back to me, "Mmmm-michael, Michael is that really you? I'm so sorry, they – he told me you were dead!" Her sobs rang through the hall. I turned to check behind me, hoping against hope that someone had crept into the room without my knowledge. My heart plummeted, every hair on the back of my neck stood up as the dread flooded into my bones. There was no-one behind me. I rolled my eyes and reluctantly turned back to face the room of expectant faces. Joe picked up on my reluctance immediately, the joy and menace shone out of his face with a malicious pleasure that illuminated it in a way I'd never seen in all the years I'd known him.

"Oh, oh this is beautiful," the wicked delight in his voice startled me into concern for this woman, "you mean – you have no idea who she is?"

I closed my eyes slowly and shook my head.

Joe's raucous laughter echoed through the cavernous main room, I knew now that my best friend of many years had gone, and in his place was this monstrous, frenzied lunatic, drunk with power. He ran around the balcony, laughing like a child at Christmas, full of eager anticipation, knowing that he had gifts waiting for him, and opening them was tantalisingly close. "You probably have questions," he sniggered, "but first, I've got some business to attend to." Without warning he withdrew an antique pistol from the holster secreted in his suit jacket, turned and fired. I flinched instinctively, half expecting to feel the unkind warmth of blood from my chest. The shock hit me harder than the bullet could've ever done, when I looked down to see my shirt, grubby but not bloodied. I looked up, relieved, but at the same time petrified, I hadn't imagined the gunshot, and if I wasn't the intended target, then…

My gaze settled on the woman who had been shepherded into the room not five minutes earlier. Her sobs had stopped, her eyes were wide with terror and pain, a trickle of blood crept from the corner of her quivering lips. The legs that had up until this point been shaky at best gave in and she collapsed to the polished metal floor. I ran to her instinctively, I didn't know why. Who she was was still a mystery to me, but we were in this nightmare together, and I couldn't watch her die alone, it was a simple human kindness to not allow that to happen. I stooped beside her and cradled her trembling body in my arms. The tears rolled down her cheeks and mingled with the blood which was now beginning to dry around her mouth. "Michael, Michael I'm so sorry," her chest heaved as she fought for her final breaths, "I never stopped, never, I've always loved you and believed that you weren't gone, I knew I'd see you again," she smiled, choking over the words which meant so much to her, "I – love – you." The final words were little more than a hushed whisper, the final remnants of air escaping her lungs, as she finished, the trembling stopped, her eyes rolled back in their sockets and her eyelids closed. Her lifeless body was cradled to my chest, which was heaving with the shock of holding an entity that, until a mere moment ago had been a person, with hopes, expectations, family and friends. Now she lay before me, a husk, everything she was had been evacuated, the very essence of her humanity trickling away with the final drops of blood. Without warning I found myself on my feet, a blind fury coursing through my veins, I leapt forwards, pushing the two guards down and away from me. I scrambled up the stairs, a high, guttural shriek, nothing was in my control, there were two more guards at the top of the stairs, I grabbed them by the collars, and pulled them over the side of the stairs, the shock in their eyes only drove me on, the dull thud and crack of their bones breaking as they hit the metal gave me a kind of exhilaration, all the while the adrenaline repressed the nausea that had risen to my throat. Joe had seen me coming, but the violence of my approach had taken him aback, the delight vanished from his face. I was on him before he could react; one punch knocked him backwards onto the console which flashed indignantly at the interruption to its programming. Dazed he looked up at me, the fear from his face gave me a dirty feeling of pleasure; I threw two more solid punches which drew blood.

"Who was she?" I screamed, the spittle flying from the corners of my mouth, mixing with the tears which I hadn't felt roll down my numb cheeks in the frenzy. I shook him by his lapels, attempting to illicit the answer to my question, "WHO?" I repeated, louder. The anger and frustration bled out of every pore. I could feel him shaking, but not with fear. The laughter bubbled up through him like a fountain. It stopped me like a punch in the gut. Temporarily confounded by his apparent lack of fear, my grip loosened; using my moment of weakness to his advantage, Joe struck like a cobra who had been playing dead until its antagonist ran out of strength and began to move on. The first punch rocked me back, a solid hook to the stomach, the two following to the head dropped me to the floor, I tasted blood. Joe's perfectly shone black shoes clattered on the metal grates on the floor as they came closer to my face. He crouched down, a slender finger under my chin forced my eyes to meet his. The eager smugness had returned, grotesquely smeared across his face, "All in good time, old friend, all in good time." He turned away; letting my head drop to the cold metal floor, bathing my cheek in my own blood, nodded to the guard who had positioned himself a few paces away. The guard stepped forward, his boot came down firmly on the side of my head and sent me sliding into a dark abyss of unconsciousness.

Chapter Eight

The ghostly faces swam through the gloom of my mind, the terrified woman, her gaze fixed firmly on me, eyes widening as the bullet penetrated her heart, Mark's pallid jowls and watery eyes, glaring witheringly. I rolled onto my side, dazed and nauseated. Groggily I opened my eyes, the green haze from my hand illuminated the windowless cell I found myself in. It was eerily terrifying, I had got used to the hue that exuded from it, but now, in this unfamiliar place, in the darkness, it seemed to add to the alien feeling I was being subjected to. I didn't matter, if I never went back to my flat, no-one would miss me. The final words of the woman who had died in my arms rang in my ears, agonisingly. She had loved me, for how long was anyone's guess. How could I know? I wasn't even certain of my own age anymore. I shut my eyes again and her face appeared, the smear of blood as prominent in my mind as it had been as she lay there dying. My eyes stung with the tears of the previous few hours, the ethereal green light not helping the sandpaper feeling which made it painful to keep them open, but I couldn't win the fatiguing battle either way, when I closed them, the face of the brutally murdered woman re-emerged. I paced round the cell, it was ten steps long, and only four wide. The oppressive walls stretched above me, looming above my head and disappearing off into the darkness. The claustrophobic room, the hunger, the lack of cigarettes and the constant green light combined to nauseate me. My mouth tasted of the dried blood from the beating that Joe had handed to me; although there was no mirror, I was certain that there were three bruises around my head, one under my left eye, ballooning upwards to close it against its will. The second followed my jawline up below my ear, it itched as if there was a cut along it, but it hurt too much to check. The final without a shadow of a doubt was the most painful of the three, the guard had been ruthless when he had stamped on my face, a tangible boot print irrevocably changed my features, my once straight nose had been cracked along the bridge, my top lip was swollen, scabbing slowly, and my forehead had gained another lump where, presumably, he had kicked me with a steel toe cap, long after my consciousness had faded.

I mused silently on the several thoughts that swam through my mind, not in any particular order, or with any sense of logic or reason. I kept them inside my head, tucked away behind my eyes, the one place I was certain Joe and these shady bastards hadn't infiltrated, at least not yet. How long had I been here? Where was here? Could I have dreamed the whole thing? If I stood up now, tried to open the door, would I be back in my flat, staring out over the field behind my bedroom, the golden light of the sun's first rays breaking free of the night's icy fist. This daydream had wasted a few moments, taking me away from the present, into a realm of fantasy, where I was still the James Bond character my ego had delighted in filling my head with, instead of this declawed lion, observed by his captors, but useless in his own habitat, unable to hunt and gain copious amounts of female attention, a dethroned king, neutered and powerless to avoid what was coming next. This thought became tangible, sticking in my throat, mixing with the ferrous stale blood into a bitter tasting combination of fear, anger and resentment. I spat on the floor, it gave me a temporary reprieve, but not long enough for my liking. All too soon it was back, snaking its way through my mouth, making me hate everything, not only the situation, but myself and everything that had happened recently. I loathed myself at the best of times, but I was carrying the weight of the murdered woman's life on my shoulders. The guilt swallowed heart downwards, spiralling through my stomach, burrowing itself further down into the swelling abyss spreading out from my gut, an ever expanding black hole, with no remorse or feeling, just an insatiable appetite, feeding on anything it came across.

Unexpectedly the door swung open and Joe, flanked by two guards, stepped in from the blinding neon strip lights in the corridor. The anger reared up through the darkness in my abdomen, flaring visibly red, a supernova, exploding in the final throes of vibrancy before being swallowed back into the darkness which would not be denied. The guards stepped the remaining nine paces to the bench on which I was now sitting, squinting as my eyes adjusted to the lighting flooding in. The rough grab of the guards on my upper arms stirred me out of the stupor I had been sitting in. They raised me to my feet, placed a bag over my head and dragged me squirming angrily from the cell.

As soon as my feet touched the polished metal of the corridor floor, I missed the close isolation of my cell. The fear flowed through me in waves, building in my stomach, rising and breaking in my throat, swallowing it back down only seemed to start the process again, but it was definitely better than the alternative of letting the overpowering nausea feeling win me over. My nostrils flared in the darkness of the bag. The warmth of my breath swirled back to me through the heavy fibres which came closer and went further away with the shallow breaths that were escaping my chest. I fought for control, the need to control my breathing and concentrate was paramount, whenever they removed the bag, I would need all my mental faculties to be working with me rather than against me to face whatever they may have in store.

Chapter Nine

I was right. I was forced into a harsh metal seat and felt the clasps of manacles close ominously around my feet. The bag was roughly dragged back over my ruined face, carpet fibres catching on the stubble on my chin, burning the open wounds which had begun to heal. I blinked in the bright light of a solitary uncovered light bulb swinging above my head. I glanced around nervously, knots of panic tightening in my chest; the oscillation of the bulb threw warped shadows onto the oddly shiny walls and table which spread out in front of me, a chessboard stood between me and the other chair. A door at the other end of the room opened. The bustling room I had entered through when I first came to this place hummed with the metronomic clatter of machinery and voices, almost rhythmically soothing. Joe stepped through the door, head slightly bowed. He watched me studiously, struggling furiously against the shackles that held me firmly in my place. “Jesus, you look like shit.” His voice had lost the insane edge it had had the last time we were in each other’s company. He strolled forwards, pulling a chair out from under the table in front of us and sitting, mere inches from me.

“Yeah? Well I’m doing a lot better than that woman you shot.” I spat, unable to keep the contempt from my voice.

He chuckled under his breath, looking at his hands, which he was massaging nervously in his lap. “Yeah, she was,” he paused, picking up a pawn from the board and twirling it in his fingers, “surplus to requirements.” The way he referred to her like a piece in the twisted game which spread out between us unnerved me, he had lost the sense that a human life had value, beyond what he needed from it. A chill shot through my spine, a reluctant acceptance that the only reason I was still alive, and being kept alive was because Joe, and this organisation, needed me for something. They would kill me as soon as they had found what it was. I held the trump card, I didn’t know what it was yet, but it was the reason I was still breathing. The realisation fired a shot of adrenaline into my system, a sudden calm focus swept over the raging storm of fear and anger that had held me under its tide since the woman had died.

Joe replaced the pawn and nodded toward the completed board. “Shall we?” his words were a question, but his tone was too firm, pushing me; it may have been a question, but there was no chance for refusal. I shrugged, heart sinking all the while.

“Excellent!” He clapped his hands once, another light came on to my left, and the reason why the walls had been shiny became clear. Mark sat in a chair behind the one way glass, clamped at the knees and ankles, arms strapped at the forearms. His head slumped forwards toward his chest, the bald patch on the back of his head reflecting the glow of the bulb above him, stripped to the waist with electrodes spanning his chest, that radiated out and down along the floor and disappeared under the glass. A shudder of foreboding ran through me like the current I could only assume was about to be fired through Mark at any opportunity. I had to be smart, figure out a way to survive, to stay alive long enough to find out why I was here, who that woman was, and most importantly, how to get out.

The pieces stood tall and silent, mine black, Joe's white. I had had no choice in which colour I got, it had already been prescribed for me, much like most of the events recently, they all had the feeling that every meticulous detail had been planned, to the second, leaving no room for error. The choice of game confused me, if every move had been planned, then why were we playing chess? After only one move each, there are over four hundred ways to play the game. If Joe had gone to so much effort to plan each stage of this, why would he give me so much scope for choice? Joe looked down at the pristine, modern board. The pieces were glass, not wood, as was the board, the black pieces represented by frosted glass, the white, clear. He made his move. "You probably have many questions," he twirled the king's pawn in his fingers before setting it down two squares from where it had started, "what is going on here, who are we, and, probably most important, why have we brought you here?" He was in no rush to answer. He had me where he wanted, and was enjoying watching me flounder in my confusion. Like an insect he was taking particular pleasure in removing the legs from. He was right, I did have those questions, but as they surfaced, they were all burned into nothingness by the one that soared above them all.

"Who was she, the woman?" I asked. My mouth was dry, making me choke over the words that caught somewhere between my throat and tongue, making me trip over them, as if I'd forgotten how to talk. Joe waved to a guard who approached, bent down to Joe's shoulder and nodded before retreating. He came back moments later, carrying a jug of water and two glasses. Thirstily I lunged for mine, the water caressing my coarse and swollen lips, downing the glass in three gargantuan gulps. Breathing heavily I looked up expectantly, toying mindlessly with a pawn. I was brought crashing out of my reverie all too soon. A sudden, high shriek startled me back to the room. I glanced to my left to see Mark convulsing wildly, the electricity clenching up his muscles with an uncontrollable spasm. Joe chuckled under his breath, "Aha, I see you've found our conundrum, a little teaser if you will." He gestured languidly towards Mark's recovering body. "You see, when you make a move, the board's pressure pads sense which piece you've moved, and where you've moved it to," he chuckled again, "and if you make a move that hasn't been set out in the computer's predetermined game, then our little nosy parker friend here gets fried like an egg!"

The blood pounded in my ears, nostrils flaring uncontrollably. I fought for control, my hands shaking as they hovered above the board. Joe's smile flickered round the corners of his mouth, "Anyway," he paused again, "the woman was part of the grander scheme of things."

I grunted, that was about as useful as a chocolate teapot when it came to information, it just meant that there was another move, a bigger plan that encompassed everything that had happened in the past few days, or however long I'd been in this hell. "Care to elaborate?"

He grinned devilishly, the malice flashing through his clear green eyes. "You were, as I'm sure nosey here told you," he gestured to Mark, "a scientific mind of unequalled power, the advances you made were revolutionary, they pushed humanity to the next stage." His face was a mixture of pride and jealousy. "Naturally there were people who would see the work you'd done used for the harm of others–"

"You, for one," I interjected sourly.

He looked taken aback, slightly offended by the very notion. Then he burst out laughing, "Of course! You didn't realise the potential as weapons your inventions possessed. The money we could've made. War is more profitable than peace, everyone could see it, and everyone still does. What we've built here is based on the foundations you started. The Phoenix project, it's called."

He glanced up, almost wary of my reaction. I just sat there, stunned. Everything around us was a perversion of an ideal; my dream of a peaceful Utopia had been cruelly snatched from me and remoulded to accommodate a more sinister end. Profit before people. It sickened me.

He continued, "The people I work for grew tired of your idealisms, and they commissioned me to engineer a takeover of the facility."

"The accident." The words were out of my mouth before I could stop them. The pieces were fitting together in my mind, twisting the final squares of the Rubik's cube together to make the story painfully obvious. I moved my queenside pawn, expecting the shocks to course through Mark's body, only to be relieved when he remained silent.

He smiled and nodded enthusiastically, moving his bishop forward, "You're getting it now, the only way to make you disappear and make it seem like an accident, was in fact, to stage an accident. We had everything set up, a secret project had been commissioned, I had to convince you to take the job, but when we were working on it, it was relatively easy to sabotage. I had fixed remote controlled explosives they supplied to the base of the project and made some excuse about not being able to be involved that night." A slight resignation entered his voice, "Just a shame really, that the moment everything had been set up, you get a telephone call that your wife had gone into labour, so were leaving as the bomb went off."

Three things leapt into my mind in an instant; Joe had been against me from the start, contorting anything I did to fit his greater plan, my wife, who was she? Why couldn't I remember her? Finally, and most importantly, she had been in labour? I was a father? The last thought stole my breath away, an excitement stirred in my chest, dousing the furnace of fear that had been raging for the most part of my imprisonment. "So what happened next?" I pushed him for answers, the excitement almost threatening to overcome me.

"You were leaving the site when the explosion happened. You saw everything and ran back towards the building. Then the fire reached the gas cylinders we used for power at the time, blew up and knocked you back from the force of the blast. You were lucky to survive, but you were in a coma for six years, before waking up and not remembering anything." He smirked with his head bowed, "In actual fact; that worked out just about as perfectly as it could have at the time. You see, I didn't want to kill you, you were my best friend, so in actual fact, you losing your memory was the perfect solution."

I groaned, my legs were stiffening in the clamps, tiredness was sinking in. I studied the board, although there were so many moves available to me this early on,

I was fully aware of what would happen if I chose the wrong one. A solitary bead of sweat made its way down my ruined forehead toward the end of my crooked nose. I glanced up before moving my knight into the game, "And my wife…" I prompted.

"She gave birth to a baby girl, Adrienne, her name was." Joe hesitated, waiting for me to catch on, almost teasing the answer from behind my eyes. Then it hit me, Adrienne – Miss A! Well, if she'd known that she was my daughter then the joke in the car about our first date was incredibly awkward.

"Miss A," I stammered.

"Exactly!" Joe exclaimed. "Your daughter came to us, we trained her up and now she's an assassin of the highest quality."

My heart sank, I'd often dreamt of a family, being able to watch a tiny human life grow and change, before sending it out into the world, ready to change it for the better; and my daughter had been wrenched away from me, God knows where her mother had been throughout all this, changed into the one thing I never would've dreamt of for any child of mine. A killer. "So where was my wife when you were corrupting my daughter?" I asked, unable to keep the fury from shaking my voice.

What happened next was completely unexpected. Joe began to laugh absolutely uncontrollably, to the point he coughed, rocking backward and forward in his seat. "That's the beauty of it," he paused to recuperate, "she needed a shoulder to cry on, when you were out of action," I didn't like where he was going with this, "and I was there to pick up the pieces, it was pretty easy, new mother, hormones all over the place, feeling abandoned, left by everyone she loved. It made it superbly easy to get into her head, then soon after, her bed." He sank back in his chair, snickering like a schoolchild who had looked up his profanity in a French to English dictionary.

A blind fury consumed me, the same feeling as when I'd seen the woman get shot. Without thinking I swept my arm across the table, knocking the chess pieces to the floor, shattering into a shower of crystalline powder. I pounded my fists into the board, shattering the glass squares until my knuckles bled. A primal scream burst from my chest, a deep growl I had no control over. I wrestled against the straps that prevented me from launching across the table and throttling Joe. He was still shaking with laughter, the control he had fed his insanity like oxygen to a fire. He danced through the shower of defunct chess pieces, making his way round the table until he was standing behind me. I felt his hands roughly take position up on my cheeks. The bruises ached where he forced the heel of his hand into them. He turned my head to the left, so I was facing Mark's window.

Mark.

I had completely forgotten about him, and as I stared on horrified, Mark's body gave up, the twitches from the shocks still making his muscles contract as his skin began to smoke slightly, the saliva hanging in strands from his twitching lips. The pre-programmed chess board must have triggered a destruct sequence when I had begun to smash it, sending it into overload, shocking Mark's body repeatedly until it finally stopped his heart. I couldn't think of many more painful ways to go. Joe released my head, I looked away, ashamed that I had let my temper get the better of me; it had resulted in the death of someone else, another person who had known me before this 'accident', someone who thought that I would know how to save them. Joe bent down to the piles of shattered glass, sifting through it to retrieve the black king. "You see," he whispered, "this, is you, the black king, with all your allies removed, you are nothing, just one piece in a wider game, a game that we, your opponents, have under control. We have removed all the pieces that were protecting you, and now," he leant in so his face was millimetres from mine, "the game is over."

He made his way briskly over to the door he had entered through. When he reached it, he turned, looked me dead in the eyes, "Oh by the way, the woman I shot," the smirk spread across his face, mixed with something which resembled pride, "was Katherine," he paused, green eyes full of malice, "our wife."

Chapter Ten

The pain swept through me like a tidal wave, my head sank down to my chest and the great, heaving sobs burst from me, sweeping away the fury, and all that was left in its place was resignation. The door behind me swung open and slammed shut, I didn't even raise my head, the guilt, anger and depression encircled me. I almost didn't feel the needle in my neck, but by the time I realised what was happening it was too late, my swollen eyelids felt heavier than they were, even with the bruising. I didn't fight them closing, drifting into an anaesthetised sleep.

The smell hit me before I even opened my eyes. I must have been back in my flat, the musty mixture of blood, cigarettes and alcohol hung in the air like a tangible grey cloud; judging by the strength of the stench, I had been away for a couple of weeks. It had lost a bit of the edge which had made Miss A, or Adrienne as I now knew, recoil, however it had gained a certain unkempt aspect which made the whole place feel as isolated and uncared for as I was. I groaned heavily, rolled over and swung my feet over the side of the bed. I felt like I had slept for weeks, months even, the sedative they had given me at the Phoenix building had rested me so well everything that had happened in the past couple of weeks felt almost like a dream; echoing through my consciousness as the shadow of someone else's memory. I rubbed my eyes, only to be greeted by the face of my wife; bleeding and broken as she had lain dying in my arms, looming out of the darkness behind my eyes.

I stumbled to the bathroom, stripped and stepped into the shower without even looking in the mirror. Regardless of how long I'd slept for, my face would still bear the healing wounds of the previous few weeks' events, and I wasn't ready to face that just yet. The water scalded down the back of my neck and, even though it was too hot, I stayed under it, the heat burning away the memories of the Phoenix building. The blood under my nails came away with a bit of persuasion, the last tactile remnants of my wife swirling down the plug hole. I put my hands to my face and felt the rough scars and cuts beneath my fingertips. I scrubbed my face hard, in the hope that somehow I would scrape away the memories of Joe, Mark, my wife, and the Phoenix building; but every time I shut my eyes, their faces danced mesmerisingly behind them. Only when I opened my eyes did they fade, leaving behind the traces of their memories, wafting away in the haze of steam and condensation that collected on the bathroom tiles. I looked down at my hands; my over-zealous scrubbing had had one definite effect. My cuts were open again; blood trickling through my fingers, diluted by the water running off the top of my head and the tears from my still moistened eyes.

I spent another twenty minutes in the shower, allowing the boiling water to mingle with the blood and tears that met on my face. Crying, numb, I stood naked, a raking pain in my chest giving a physical characteristic to the torment in my mind. I couldn't wrap my mind around any of what had happened, I had witnessed my best friend, or so I thought, murder my wife, who I had no idea had existed, whilst my daughter watched on with no emotion in her face. All of this was so twisted; I was being swept away by a wave of utter lunacy, drowning with no sign of rescue.

I stepped out of the shower, drying my face gingerly, trying to make sure none of the towel's fibres became attached to the newly re-opened cuts. As I finished the routine, a thought hit me, as though it had been dropped from above into the furrows of my brain. A kernel of an idea that took root almost instantly, sprouting a green shoot which pushed its way forward, making it impossible to concentrate on much else. "*I've got to cut the head off the snake. If Joe wants a war, that's what he'll get.*"

Chapter Eleven

My stomach gave a low rumble which reminded me I hadn't eaten since I'd woken up. I stumped into the kitchen and opened the fridge. A low sigh escaped my chest; there was nothing in there, nothing edible at least. I trudged back to my bedroom, changed, picked up my cigarettes, keys, and phone and left my flat. I wandered through the early spring mid-morning, the sun was soothing and warm, chasing away the late winter chill which had lingered in the crisp morning breeze. I wasn't walking with any purpose, just being out in the fresh air was cleansing to my spirit. My stomach gave another, longer rumble, reminding me of the reason behind this jaunt out. I walked to the local café and stepped inside. I didn't eat the first fry-up placed in front of me, so much as inhale it, and was on my way to order a second when I caught sight of the tall, well-dressed man, in the same suit as before, striding into the café, on the security camera screen behind the counter.

The chill of fear shot up my spine, the piercingly blue eyes loomed out at me from the screen. I tapped on the counter, betraying the nerves that were racing round my system. This was only the second time I'd seen him in real life, all the other interactions we had previously had been inside my mind. The clatter of his pointed shoes on the tiled floor of the greasy spoon alerted me to his approach. All too soon he was standing behind me, calmly waiting as if he were just another customer coming in from the cold. A hearty British breakfast, tea and browse of a tabloid before heading to another day in an office, filing reports and working on spreadsheets. His unassuming aura terrified me. The control of the situation was completely in his hands, as if somehow all this was pre-determined. Regardless of what I was thinking of doing, every outcome had been accounted for and factored in, no doubt all the exits were covered, who knows, perhaps even a few of the other customers were in on this. The touch on my shoulder had come all too soon, my mind had slipped away from me, leaving me blinded in the dust of confusion. I could almost feel the colour draining from my face, draining into an icy pool at the pit of my stomach. There was no way that this situation ended well for me. Numbly I turned to face him, he was taller than I had imagined, slender and even more imposing. The piercing blue eyes stared down sternly from their lofty position above the well-appointed nose and mouth, which pursed slightly at the corners as he began to speak. "Michael, you need to come with me now," he began.

"And why would I do that?" I retorted sharply.

"Well basically, we've got all the exits covered, five of the seven patrons in here are actually with me, and, here's the main thing," he paused, "if you try to run, even though we're not allowed to kill you, we could make it an incredibly painful travelling experience for you."

I shrugged, the facial expression of resignation which spread across my face made the slightly healed cuts twinge and burn, reminding me of the last time I tried going against people who were out to get me. Almost making my mind up for me. “Fine,” I murmured angrily.

Head down, I stomped out of the café and was greeted by the yawning unwelcoming doors of an unmarked black van. The doors snapped shut, like the yawning jaws of a crocodile, trapping the bewildered wildebeest and beginning the death rolls. The engine sputtered into life and the van pulled away slowly at first, then gathering speed as we headed further from the café, further from home, further from safety.

The journey seemed to go on for an eternity, the sharp breaths of panic emanating from my chest echoed out through the silence. Fighting for control, my eyes began to adjust to the gloom. I was alone in the back of the van; there was nothing there to even suggest who these people were, what they wanted or even where we were going. A surge of frustration hit me. All that had happened in the past few weeks could have been going on for years with me blissfully unaware, living in a dreamy haze of alcohol and tobacco, without me ever needing to know. My wife would’ve still been alive, saddened but alive nonetheless. I’d have been alone, without any knowledge that I had a daughter, and that my daughter had become an assassin, who would have no qualms about killing me if the orders came through from above, from the man I used to consider my best friend. I swallowed the nausea that rose in my throat. The van had stopped moving whilst I was lost in my thoughts, the engine idled quietly. We had arrived.

Chapter Twelve

The heavy stomp of boots quickened my pulse and shortened my breaths. The fear was holding me in a trance. There would almost certainly be too many to overpower on my own, especially without anything I could use as a makeshift weapon. Resigned to the fact that I'd have to go along with these people, whoever they were, yet again no choice was afforded to me, I stood up, head bowed, and waited for the doors to reveal my captors.

The guards had formed a tight semi-circle around the back of the van, rifles all pointing inwards; ensuring that one false move, one attempt to run would by my final action on this earth. Adrienne flitted nervously around behind them, her tension almost palpable as she darted back and forth behind the guards. "Something's got her rattled," I thought, "good." It wasn't that I wanted to see my daughter in any kind of distress, but the idea that something had shaken her resolve and her belief in her employers.

"Get him out of there," she commanded, managing to keep the authority in her voice even if her movement betrayed her nerves, "move it!"

Two guards stepped forward into the back of the van, clipping handcuffs tightly around my wrists, "Oh, kinky," I said, looking one of the guards dead in the eyes, "at least buy me a drink first!" That earned me a swift jab in the ribs with the butt of his gun before they manoeuvred me out into what I could now see was an abandoned hangar. The skeletal frames of old aircraft loomed from each side. This was definitely a graveyard of some kind or another. All the comfort of seeing Adrienne tense had vanished in an instant. What if it wasn't just planes that were disposed of here? How could I even contemplate an escape without being instantly gunned down by the hoard of guards? They swarmed over the hangar floor like a colony of ants, busily maintaining the nest, while the queen sits in residence somewhere on high, unseen.

This musing had left me standing a little too long for the guard's liking, another firm prod and a terse "Move!" brought me back to earth with a jolt.

I lumbered forward, flanked by four guards on either side, Adrienne strolling a little more confidently just over my right shoulder. The labyrinth of corridors had obviously been re-worked by the current occupants, the walls, floors and ceilings were a bright, pearlescent white, which glared with the reflection of the powerful bulbs which were inlaid into the sides of the floors. We walked for what felt like hours, although, when you're afraid, even though your heart can be racing, the world around you seems to slow to an almost torturous pace. We arrived at a large metal door with bolts running all round its edge and a heavy wheel in the centre. It was an ominous looking door, the type that wouldn't have looked out of place in a maximum security prison or bank vault. A shudder of fear and foreboding shot through me like an icy dagger. Whatever was behind that door was not going to be puppies and candy floss.

As two of the guards stepped forward and began busying themselves with the weighty door I chanced a look over my shoulder at Adrienne. She was standing about two feet away from me, arms behind her back, eyes darting up and down the corridor we had just walked down, as if she was expecting some unwelcome company. When she wasn't scanning our surroundings she stared at the floor, avoiding the eyes of everyone in the posse which had shepherded me from the van to this point.

The two guards had finished opening the door. All eyes were now on me, for the third time a jab in the ribs and the command of "Move" made me stumble forward into the gloom.

This corridor was much smaller and narrower than before, almost like a prison cell, with only room for Adrienne and one of the guards from my welcoming committee and me. The heavy door swung shut with a dull clunk, pitching the three of us into total darkness. The sole source of light came from the green chip in the back of my hand, casting an eerie green glow over all the occupants of this holding area. Moments later the far panel of the corridor slid back with a pneumatic hiss to reveal a spacious, antiquated room, with high, wing chairs, and a wide hearth which crackled with the heat of the logs burning merrily away inside it. It was strange, had it not been for the death star style corridors outside I'd have happily been quite comfortable in this room, which, for its part was the only thing in this whole hangar which felt more out of place than me. All the light came from a large window which overlooked the cracked tarmac of the defunct runway. Silently, Adrienne nodded to one of the wing chairs that encircled the dark mahogany desk, behind which the man from the café sat, totally relaxed, surveying his guests with a calm, icy glare, made even more piercing by his pale blue eyes.

"Ah Michael, come, sit down, so glad we could finally meet, drink?" The jovial tone of his voice took me aback, up until now in every vision he had appeared in, he had spoken in an almost monotone, as if the outside world was somehow so mundane it did not require his full and undivided attention. This was his den, his comfort zone, the place he could be completely at ease, only a few hundred miles away from civilisation and behind military grade security.

"Water," I grunted.

My answer seemed to startle him slightly, he replaced the decanter of scotch he had produced from a drawer in the desk and signalled to the guard, who turned back through the door we had come through in the hunt for a tap.

"So you're probably wondering why we had to bring you here, and under such subterfuge," he began, a boyish excitement bubbling through him.

"No not really, the whole guns and vans thing has been a bit over played for me at the moment." I said in the same monotone voice he was so adept at employing, locking unblinking eyes with him.

He allowed himself a disconcerting giggle. It was the same insane snort of laughter Joe had let slip moments before he shot my wife. I shifted uncomfortably in the plush seat.

"Years ago, while you were in your coma, the Phoenix project was dead in the water, we had no idea if Joe's plan to usurp you had worked. So we made contingency plans," he paused, eying me with glee, trying to gauge my reaction before continuing, "a sample of your DNA was taken and used to fertilise an egg we had obtained, and, using cloning techniques that were even beyond the government's best minds of the day, we developed an identical clone."

"So you're telling me that years before Government scientists even attempted to clone a sheep, you lot, whoever you are, were knocking out perfect human clones?" I laughed, "You're either a bullshitter, or insane, or even an insane bullshitter, and on the past few weeks' evidence I can't spot those fuckers. Who knows?"

A foolish grin spread across his face, "Well I'm not, as you put it, bullshitting you, so what options does that leave?" He made direct eye contact for the first time in this exchange, icy blue meeting muddy brown.

"Well, it means you're one nugget short of a happy meal at best," I snorted.

"Your scepticism is amusing." He leant back, straightening his tie and smoothing his charcoal black suit.

A flourish of his right hand to a camera secreted in the far corner and the door slid open again, I heard the footsteps of the latest incumbent enter the room. I craned my neck around the corner of the chair only to recoil in shock. The shoes were the first thing I noticed. Battered black leather size eights, the suit clad the more muscular frame and the face was no longer as weathered or drastically aged, no scars or stubble, but it was definitely me, without a shadow of a doubt. It was terrifying; the glimpse behind the curtain into a parallel world. My eyes met my eyes, only for a second, I couldn't hold it. "Fuck," I sputtered. There were no words for this situation, until a few weeks ago I was completely alone, now there were two of me. I stood, numb. I circled him in disbelief, me mk. two. The antique clock on the wall hammering away the minutes in the silence, one circuit of him was plenty for me; I could feel the heat behind my eyes of the shocked tears I was fighting back. "No fucking way, this is insane, it's a mask or something, it has to be!" I leapt back to mk. two and started clawing at his neckline, pulling the tie away and scraping my fingernails at his throat. He took a shocked step back, the violence of my sudden outburst left marks on his neck, but no tell-tale tears in latex. I fell to my knees, the adrenaline leaving the hollow sting of resignation. The tears I had been holding back broke past the dam my mind had been busily constructing, cries so anguished I could almost feel the blue eyed man's hand wrenching my heart from my chest. This wasn't some sick dream, or hallucination, this was real. They had made a carbon copy of me, taken my identity, my intellect, but moulded him to their will, if they had told him to make a bomb, I felt certain he wouldn't have my moral squirming in the pit of his stomach as he set about constructing something which would make a nuclear bomb look like a firecracker.

"Now," the nameless man began, "your re-emergence into this world has presented us with a slight quandary. We had planned on introducing your clone here as you to the world, spearheading our new, exciting project under your name. But now, what to do…" He sucked his teeth, ponderously. His cold eyes pitilessly flicked from my crumpled, kneeling and sobbing frame to one of the people behind me, either Adrienne or mk. two. "Kill him." His merciless command made me look up, straight into his icy stare.

"As you wish," Adrienne replied coolly from behind me.

"No, wait, please!" I blurted out. I never thought it would end like this, me, begging for life on my knees.

Her footsteps drew closer, I counted my breaths, wondering which one of them would be my last, shorter and sharper with every step. I closed my eyes, held my breath and waited. The bullet hissed from the silenced muzzle of the pistol, and with a thud, a body hit the floor.

I twisted my neck round so fast my head spun. Lying on the floor in an ever expanding pool of his own blood was mk. two, my brown eyes glassy and unfocused as the bullet wound in his forehead as the remnants of his life trickled away.

"NO!" The angry cry of the blue-eyed man stopped me from staring at my own corpse, "You were meant to kill the other one!" he screeched.

"You didn't specify," came the cool response.

Without another word, the blue-eyed man scrabbled for, presumably, a gun in his desk drawer. Adrienne moved faster than I had seen anyone ever move, she almost flitted momentarily from where she was to behind him. Withdrawing a long, slender knife from her belt she took hold of a clump of his hair and in one swift flash of steel drew her knife along his throat. The warm blood showered the antiquities in the room and me alike, covering everything in a fine red mist, which hung in the air for a second before landing softly on every surface in the room.

"Come on!" she yelled. I knelt there, frozen in shock and terror; in the space of a few minutes I had seen my daughter murder two people in front of me, without a second glance. Still in complete shock I stood. From another holster Adrienne produced another gun, this one with a grapple-hook protruding from the barrel. I was standing beside her as she aimed it toward the rusted water tower on the other side of the nearest runway. As we were preparing to be pulled through the window, the door swept open, guards piled in from the corridor guns at the ready. In that moment the line engaged and we shot forward, a hail of bullets buzzing like an angry swarm of wasps around us. “Grab a grenade off my belt,” yelled Adrienne over the clatter of gunfire. Hurriedly I fumbled with her belt, finding the round, palm sized explosive. I pulled the pin out with my teeth and hurled it back through the jagged glass of the window. The whole room erupted in a brilliant orange fireball which leapt from the window pursuing us and hurling debris from the exploding room as we made our escape to the top of the water tower.

Atop the tower, we could see the smoke billowing from the crater in the side of the building where the bodies of mk. two and the blue eyed man had been neatly disposed of. My heart rate still hadn’t returned to normal, I could hear each and every beat thundering in my ears, making my whole head throb nauseatingly. I sat on the rusted corrugated roof of the tower and looked up at Adrienne. Her calm aura soothed me slightly, the adrenaline ebbed away gradually as the breeze caressed my cheek. As it did so, a pain in my left arm sprung up like a fountain. I fumbled with the back of my bicep which felt oddly warm and sticky. I brought my fingers in front of my face to see they were covered in blood. I glanced up toward Adrienne, whose eyes widened with momentary shock as she saw the crimson on my fingertips.

“Dad?” she crouched by my side.

“What?” I was briefly taken aback by someone calling me ‘Dad’ for the first time. Even though it came out of the mouth of someone I hadn't known all that long, it felt right, as if she was the right person to say it and I was the only one who she should ever be able to say it to. "How did you know I was your Dad?" I frowned.

"The chess match, behind the glass," she started, "Joe didn't know I was there, and when the room was empty I took some of your DNA to compare to mine."

"Suddenly everyone's got a copy of my DNA," I grunted belligerently.

"I'm sorry Dad," Adrienne mumbled, "had I known that they had taken anything from you, I'd have contacted you sooner."

I shrugged, I felt sorry for her, if her mother had thought that I was dead, then she would have told her daughter so at the appropriate point, she wasn't to know that I existed, or even that a clone of me existed. "Don't worry about it."

She visibly relaxed after hearing that. "So when the DNA results came back and I knew for certain I was your daughter, I had to get you away from this, it's dangerous Dad, and if they think you're coming back, they'll kill you, and me, and speed up their plans."

"Plans, what plans?" I asked, brow furrowed.

"I can't tell you any more, not here at least, you never know who could be listening," she said. The regret was etched into every syllable.

That made sense, they could have bugged her, or both of us, or heard about this escapade and would be after us by now.

"It's ok, I understand," I said, "can we–" I gestured to my arm, "I mean, this really fucking hurts."

She nodded silently, and fished out a communicator from one of the pockets on her jacket. "Miss A here, come in Alpha squad." She paused for a moment, the voice crackled through the static on the other end. "Ok, message received and understood, rendezvous in ten minutes." With that she clicked off the communicator and turned back to me. "Ok Dad, we're going to be picked up by a helicopter in ten minutes, when they arrive, we'll have medical supplies enough to get that sorted. Keep your hand on it now."

I nodded tiredly; the blood loss was competing with the nauseated feeling for total control of my emotions, caught between sickness and light-headed dizziness brought about by the blood loss. I clutched my arm. The next thing I remember was the whirr of the helicopter rotors blasting the air into my face. Hazily I gazed up as I was lifted by four guards into the rear of the chopper. The sharp jab of the needle brought everything out of soft focus; Adrienne sat close to my head as the doctor busied himself with the wound in my arm. I relaxed back, allowing the floating sensation of the morphine flowing through my veins to take me away from the helicopter and the pain.

Chapter Thirteen

The breath on my cheek woke me gently; the softness of the pillows I found myself on momentarily confused me. This definitely wasn't my flat, the clean, fresh scent of non-stale air swirled through the open, white-walled room. Gradually, my eyes adjusted to the brightness which flooded in through the floor to ceiling windows which lined the wall to my left. The silhouette of whoever's breath had been on my cheek was cut out against the nearest panel of glass. As she came closer the silhouette gained more defined features. Adrienne moved closer, her eyes intently sweeping over me, the relief was undeniable.

"Good morning Dad," she smiled, almost laughing with relief.

"Hey," I replied, groggily.

"How are you feeling?"

The question brought back the memory of the helicopter, the bullet, the blood. A burning sensation shot through my arm, beginning high on my bicep and spreading rapidly downward toward my hand. The hand which had, until I woke up this time, glowed with a jade green luminescence. My heart quickened as I sat up in the enormous bed. A huge scar ran parallel to my knuckles along the back of my hand, and, where the green glow had once been, now only the crimson scab which had begun to form along the incision remained.

"Fine," I replied, confused, "what happened here?" I gestured to my hand.

She paused, the relief replaced by a momentary lapse in her composure. She settled herself in the chair again, looked me in the eyes, took a deep breath and continued. "You don't know what that thing in your hand was, do you Dad?"

I hesitated; Joe had mentioned it briefly, something about it being a change, but a change in what? "No, I haven't really managed to get any answers so far, people have mentioned it. Mark and Joe for example, but they were pretty sketchy on the details."

She nodded, "Well, let me fill in some blanks for you." She fished out a thick, brown paper clad file with a white string around it. It landed at the foot of my bed with a dull thump, muffled by the soft, thick duvet. With a groan I leant forward, the roughness of the aged paper met with the cracked and peeling skin of my fingertips as I picked it up and cradled it on my knees. A plume of dust flew up from the cover as I began to skim over the blueprints, documents and letters which sprawled out of the folder, like a long lost treasure trove giving up the secrets it had long since kept buried.

I hesitated over a list of codes which caught my attention, at the top of a blueprint, dated 1978. There was an image of a chip, scaled up from millimetres to be seen in more detail. Below the date, the heading read, "ComChip Mk I manual over-ride procedure number 27953114810010146. Restricted access."

I glanced up from the page, "Restricted access? Restricted to who?" I asked, almost knowing the answer.

“The access codes for the ComChip’s remote access features were supposed to be secret to only those in the upper ranks of the Phoenix,” Adrienne began. “You were one of the people who opposed the idea, in theory it could be used to control the user in a temporary state of hypnosis almost. It was dangerous, in the wrong hands.” I grunted, I got the feeling I’d had dealings with the wrong hands recently; they belonged to my once best friend for one. “Joe,” Adrienne continued, “Joe was the one who pushed for remote access in the ComChip, on the grounds that if the chip malfunctioned inside the user, it could be shut off remotely before doing permanent damage to the neurological or immune systems.”

I hesitated, it didn’t make sense, Joe was a sociopath, it had become clear in the way he killed Mark and my wife without a second’s thought, why would he be arguing on the side of public safety? I made this remark aloud, under my breath as the dread snaked its way into my stomach. Adrienne shrugged, either unknowing or unwilling to let me enquire any further she rose from her seat, told me to get some more rest, removed the file from my lap and swept hurriedly out of the room. Reluctantly I flopped back onto the pillows which cradled my neck comfortingly as I drifted off into a comfortable sleep for the first time in years.

Chapter Fourteen

When I awoke the musty, unloved smell was back. Without even opening my eyes I could tell I was in my own flat, the stale cigarette and whiskey smell hung in the air, comforting, but disappointing, I was no longer with Adrienne. Whatever had happened to her after our last conversation could have been serious; if Joe discovered who she was with, what she had said, he would kill her. The panic hung like a stalactite over my heart, ready to fall and pierce it the instant my fears were confirmed. With a slight complaining twinge from beneath the bandage on my arm I propped myself up in the bed, lit a cigarette, and reached into the drawer for the black book I had started when the code had appeared in my mind. Hastily I scrawled out the notes of what I could remember of the previous encounters, the café, Mk II, the blue-eyed man, Adrienne's revelations and the ComChip. That green glow, the way the blue-eyed man had been able to contact me directly as if he had actually been sitting behind my eyes the whole time. A sickening punch of dread hit my guts, maybe that was the reason Adrienne had to remove the chip after the battle in the hangar office, if there had been any way of watching the events through my eyes, the likelihood would be that whoever was observing would know that I was still alive, instead of Mk II.

The existence of my clone confused me, why was he needed? Surely it wasn't just some experiment into human cloning; they needed him to replace me somehow, but why? How did they keep the cloning process away from the public gaze? There would have been prototypes before they attempted to create my doppelganger, to ensure there could be no failures in the process. I smiled; they obviously hadn't banked on my daughter knowing who I was. That was something, a small victory, whatever their plan had been it might take them a while to re-structure, especially after the death of the blue-eyed man, whoever he had been.

Feeling a little more optimistic about the next move, I swung my legs over the side of the bed, took a final drag on the gradually extinguishing cigarette, stubbed it out and headed for the bathroom. The morning shave took longer than it had habitually, after all, the scars and cuts along the beard line had made the skin as delicate as wet paper, breaking down and revealing the reddened, newer skin developing beneath. I wiped the trickle of blood from my cheek, rinsed my face, straightened up and dried off.

In the kitchen, the low growl from my stomach reminded me I hadn't eaten in hours. Reluctantly I opened the door of the fridge and stepped back as the scent of putrid milk and rotten eggs hit me like a tidal wave. I held back the heavy rising sensation of the vomit in my throat, damn, I thought, time to trawl through the supermarket.

I hated the supermarket. The fluorescent lights, the piped music that did anything but calm and the children screaming at their parents for not getting the chocolate flavour cereal their sugar-addled brains craved. I stopped and stared at the situation around me. A mother glided down an aisle ahead of me, she was as dishevelled as I was. Her small son tugged relentlessly at her sleeve. She wasn't just ignoring him; her eyes were glazed over, as if the whole necessity for food which had brought her here was merely a process that needed fulfilling. Her boy begged her for a crumb of attention, only to have it rejected. Her hand glowed blue from the chip in the back of it. My stomach twisted as I watched her. She was not in any control, the blue chip in her hand rendering her as devoid of emotion as any of the drones milling about in Joe's control centre.

I stomped head down from one aisle to another, the change rattling in my pockets, my dishevelled appearance silencing both whiny children and exhausted parents as I trudged past. After what seemed like an eternity, I stumbled through my front door laden down with flimsy plastic bags; once again having neglected to remember the mass of so called 'bags for life' that oozed out of my imaginatively named 'bag cupboard' before I embarked on the trek through the floodlit netherworld.

Fourteen minutes later, and after having eaten a substantial amount of what should've been a week's worth of shopping, I slouched languidly into the living room, flopped heavily down on the sofa, lit a cigarette and flicked through the channels of the television. I retreated to my bedroom to recover the notebook and pen I had stashed in the drawer before my first encounter with Adrienne. I stomped back into the living room as the television flicked onto a local news report. Joe stood in his dark suit, towering over the reporter who was visibly nervous about the interview. Joe's steely cool exuded from every pore, the early spring gusts that tousled the hair of the reporter barely even seemed to faze him as he waited patiently for the first question.

"So, you join me here outside the Queen Victoria hotel, with Joseph Goulder, head of the Phoenix Foundation, ahead of their annual masquerade fundraiser." A flurry of questions burst into my head, the Phoenix Foundation? How was Joe able to get onto the national news so easily? I shuddered, the nervous nausea returning to my throat, the influence of the Phoenix must be far more than I could have ever thought possible.

"Mr Goulder, it has been several months since the disappearance of Mark Walton, a former employee of the Foundation, have you anything to say on the matter?" The journalist flicked a wayward strand of wavy blonde hair out of her eyes and stared upward at Joe, who craned his neck down to stare down his nose at her, a faint smile playing in the corners of his eyes.

"Naturally, we are all concerned about Mr Walton's disappearance; as far as all of us were aware he was a kind, caring co-worker who never had shown any signs of being mixed up in anything which could have led to him being targeted for abduction." A smug smile flickered in the corners of his eyes. He was getting away with this outright lie, and laughing about it. The fury boiled in my blood, but I couldn't look away, transfixed by the screen and what might be said next. The reporter began again, "As I've said already, it's the annual masquerade ball in honour of the foundation's founder, Michael Wolf, on the anniversary of his death in an explosion many years ago." A chill shot through me, all these years they had been using me as a pin-up for all the monstrous acts committed in the name of "Phoenix", the face to the name. It was perfect, tell the people the founder was dead then say that you're continuing the work he started, without any chance he could come back and clear his name.

Well, almost perfect.

My next move was clear. I had to get into this ball. Three clear raps at the front door broke me out of this train of thought. Slowly and suspiciously I edged off the sofa, nervously making my way towards the door. The images of the last time anyone had knocked on my door flashed through my mind. My wife's shuddering final breaths, Mark's juddering body as the electricity sapped the final dregs of existence from his corpse and Joe's delighted laughter as the life had left them both. The doorknob felt cold under my numb fingers.

A flood of delighted relief tinged with confusion washed over me as I swung back the door to reveal a large cardboard box and no sign of who had delivered it. I crouched over it, my heart pounding in my ears. I glanced furtively up and down the corridor, hoping against hope I'd see a door close or the back of whoever had delivered this mystery package to my door. Turning my attention back to the box, I put my ear to the lid, with no idea what I was listening for. Satisfied that my completely unscientific check for bombs or other such articles of potential doom had been cleared, I picked it up and carried it inside. Nervously I placed it on my coffee table, mind thundering like a freight train. With trembling fingers I fumbled with the parcel tape and pulled apart the cardboard. Neatly folded atop the table was a black, classic looking tuxedo along with an intricately decorated porcelain full-face mask.

I scrabbled around on the floor to see if there had been any clue as to who had left this package, and why they had done so. Sure enough, underneath the table, a pristine white piece of paper gleamed folded in the murky dust that covered the long-neglected carpet. I stooped low and plucked it from the floor. Opening it slowly I scanned the face of the paper with a nervy glance. The only words printed on the pristine white sheet in a bold, uninspiring font read:

"It's time."

Underneath the chilling message was an elaborately decorated invitation, about the same size as a postcard, embossed with a golden Phoenix that sprawled majestically over the cover. Turning it swiftly over, I flung the dust scooped from the carpet into my face. Choking through the haze of cigarette ash and crushed insect corpses flung up from the floor, I began scanning over the neatly inscribed invite.

You are cordially invited to the Michael Wolf Memorial ball on behalf of the Phoenix foundation.

8.30 pm – midnight.

As I read the invitation, the blood began to boil in my veins, "the Michael Wolf memorial?" What the hell? They were using my name to pedal this shit onto the public? I didn't believe it when it was just on the television, but now I had the invite flicking between my fingers it had become all too real. The insult burned in my stomach, a sickening fury that twisted and writhed in the deepest recesses of my guts. Now I knew the meaning of the note, now it made complete sense. The revelation was the next step.

Chapter Fifteen

The rest of the day passed in a numb blur, the tuxedo hung on the back of my bedroom door, looming over my bed like a spectre, filling my vision as I stared blankly into space, twirling the invite idly through my fingers. The sun began to sink below the horizon, throwing a golden hue into the room, and making the shadowy tuxedo even more ominous. The mask lay on the bed beside me; I glanced down at it, the sequinned border reflecting the dusk's reddish glow. I felt a deep, eerie calm, as if even nature was holding its breath; watching, waiting.

The shudder of foreboding ran through me as I stood up from the bed, reached out and touched the suit. This wasn't a good idea, I was sure of it, but what other choice did I have? I had to make it clear that none of what Joe and his cronies had done with the Phoenix had been in my name, the imprisonments, the murders. I knew it was a risk, I could easily become another victim, mercilessly snuffed out on Joe's way to… to what? World domination? Even for the power crazed lunatic he was, surely the desire for dominion over all things was something that only ever featured in spy movies? As I twisted the final buttons of the tuxedo shirt around my throat, the thought crossed my mind that had I not spent a few months imprisoned at the Phoenix base being beaten and starved I'd not fit into this suit. A smile crawled reluctantly to the corners of my lips, that was something to thank Joe for I supposed. With grim apprehension I picked up the mask through the eyeholes, took a generous swig of whiskey from the bottle on the bedside table and headed out into the dark spring evening.

The cool chill of the night's air swirled around my face as I approached the pillared entrance way of the Queen Victoria hotel. The light from the foyer spilled out down the steps and into the street. Before I was caught by the warm glow from inside, I slipped the mask down over my face, ensuring that the majority of my face was covered, took a final deep calming breath of the cool early night air, and stepped inside.

The brightness of the high ceilinged reception area took me aback, fortunately my eyes adjusted relatively quickly and, looking around, revealed that I was accompanied by a silent vigil of darkened faces, the grief etched into every line on every face. In many of the hands were small photographs of people, smiling, young, happy faces which contrasted sharply with the fear and sadness on the faces of the people holding them. As I looked closer I realised that I had seen the people in the photographs before, the 'drones' as I had called them at Joe's base; they looked more tired and strained, as if their very essence had been drained from them and all that was left was a shell, controlled ruthlessly by Joe and the Phoenix, but they were definitely the same people. My pulse quickened. What should I do? These people needed answers, some crumb of comfort; the knowledge that their loved ones were alive at the very least, surely they'd want to know that? As these thoughts crossed my mind I had to dismiss them. I really had nothing to tell them, they were alive, but where they safe? Could I tell them for certain that Joe was keeping them well, that he would let them go eventually? If I were to tell them one thing, it would just lead to more questions, questions I had no way of knowing the answers to. Resigned to the fact that my presence would do these people more harm than good, I sighed, walked past the silent mourners and into the main ballroom.

The glass panelled doors opened onto a large, bright airy room, illuminated by a mammoth crystal chandelier, which caught the light of the candles within it and threw droplets of light onto the walls. I smirked below the mask; for all the grandeur of the place, the chandelier was just a posh disco-ball. But nothing in this room was what it was pretending to be, Joe stood on the balcony that encircled the ballroom floor, drinking in the adoration of the masked crowd. Accompanying him on the balcony, Adrienne looked down on the sea of shrouded faces, her violet hair and gown shimmering in the candlelight, the smile on her face covering for the fervent flicker of her eyes from face to face, until her eyes rested on me. The relief in her eyes was clear, the warm floating sensation in my chest when her eyes met mine made me feel a little easier about being here. At least someone was glad to see me. Continuing my survey of the balcony, it became clear to me that the people flanking Joe and Adrienne must be important to the organisation, all together, here, in the open. Adrienne's message, the latest puzzle piece fell into place, this was probably the one time this year all the main heads of the Phoenix were together.

The bolt of inspiration struck like lightning. This was it, the golden opportunity. In front of all the leaders and a room full of witnesses I could remove Joe from the pedestal he had constructed for himself, pull the carpet from beneath him and leave him alone in the wilderness of excommunication.

Now all I had to do was pick my moment.

Joe stepped forward into the spotlight that illuminated a Phoenix shaped lectern which protruded out from the balcony over the polished mahogany floor of the ballroom. The smug smile from the television interview was fixed in position, the devilish twinkle once again in his emerald eyes. "Welcome friends, I'm so glad you could join us here tonight," he began, attempting to make eye contact with everyone in the room. He cleared his throat and continued, "We're gathered here to mark the twelfth year of the passing of our founder and one of the greatest innovators of his generation in an explosion, Michael Wolf." A murmur of reverie spread through the assembled crowd. I smirked beneath the mask, waiting for his spurious bullshit to reach a crescendo before I'd pounce. Joe drew a long shuddering breath; the false anguish of simulated grief covered his face better than any mask in the room, and continued. "This year, we are continuing to roll out the ComChip 2, the next stage of our drive to connect everyone, everywhere." A smattering of polite applause drowned out my snort of derision. Joe paused, allowed the applause to die down before continuing, "Thank you, thank you, now, on with the notices of the year." He paused again, surveying the upturned masked faces gazing toward him, hanging on his every word, "We are all saddened to report that our employee and friend to many here Mark Walton has died, after disappearing three months ago." The reverie returned to the mood of the room, heads bowed for moment, before reverting back to gazing on the podium from which Joe spoke. I shook my head, mimicking the saddened movements of the assembled crowd, outwardly sympathising with their loss whilst at the same time displaying my disbelief that Joe was getting away with this audacious level of deception. He cleared his throat loudly before continuing, "Also, I have suffered great personal loss this year," he faltered, "Katherine – my wife," he muttered, voice stumbling over the words, "sadly passed away in an accident six months ago." A hushed murmur of reverence spread throughout the assembled crowd.

"BASTARD." The single word spat from my lips and floated under the chin of my mask before I could stop it. Joe's face dropped as the two syllables reached him high above my head. He shuffled nervously from one foot to the other before looking round to the dignitaries, who had been sharing uncomfortable glances behind his back before fixing his gaze on me.

"I don't know who you are," he began.

"Bullshit you don't!" I snarled. My hand swiped up toward my mask, ripping it from my face and hurling it on the floor, where it shattered and scattered to the perimeter of startled onlookers which had begun to form around me. The rumble of disconcerted voices joined together and hummed around my ears like an aggravated swarm of bees, only to be silenced as they realised who I was. "You killed her, shot her right in front of me. I see her face, her blood on my hands as she died in my arms. SHE WAS MY WIFE TOO!"

The low hum of the conversations from the masked crowd stopped as though someone had flicked a switch; the shocked hush crashed about my ears like silent waves. The only sound was the tapping of Joe's fingers on the lectern. All eyes were fixed on him, his disconcerting smile back in place, as if my revelation and subsequent outburst were trivial, and nothing and no-one was going to spoil this party for him. A chuckle began to stir in his belly, I could see it, moving slowly toward his mouth, up through his chest, making his whole frame shudder, the way it had in the moments before he had killed my Katherine.

The childish giggle escaped his frame, bubbling up from his pulpit and reverberating around the high, domed ornate ceiling. His laughter had distracted me from the movements of the other guests, who had all closed ranks around me, forming a tight perimeter about three paces from where I was standing. The flickering chandelier light glittered off the porcelain masks which formed a sea, steadily encroaching inward, until all the shadows merged into one, looming over me, the bright white faces shimmering through the gloom. I took one final desperate look toward the balcony to see Adrienne being forcefully and hurriedly swept away by a burly security guard, before the encircling crowd forced me to the floor and closed off the ring of light above me.

The clawing hands of the faceless horde began to reach into the space previously only inhabited by shadows, gripping tightly to my arms and legs, clasping me firmly as, unseen high above my head, Joe's shrill, bone-chilling laughter reverberated around the dome. They forced me to my knees, fists crashing in as hands tore fervently at my clothes and skin. As every face came closer, I could see that each and every one of them had the same clouded look in their eyes. The look of the drones I had seen working in the Phoenix building, as if they were merely marionettes controlled by an evil puppeteer whose evil cackle was providing the background to my beating. I resigned myself to the torrent of fists and feet. It wasn't their fault, something or someone was controlling them, removing their conscience and self-determination, leaving them hollow and without personality. The only anger I felt was aimed at the cackling demon that ran excitedly along his balcony, surveying the scene below him in a joyous frenzy. I would get him for this, and for all the people here, who had had their lives taken from them, for Katherine, Mark and Adrienne, along with the countless people who had been, or would be indirectly affected by his lunacy. This thought strengthened me through a few more punches before the constant strikes began to wear down my resolve and draw blood. The darkness crept in from the corners of my eyes, slowly drawing me closer to restful unconsciousness. Before the final punch was thrown, a shattering sound emanated from the back of the hall as the silent protestors from the foyer burst in, smashing the doors to the ballroom. I tried to stay awake, to keep fighting as they battled their way through the crowd, but a final blow to the side of my head jolted my neck and sent me reeling back into the darkness.

Chapter Sixteen

The dark and dreamless sleep lasted for what felt like an eternity; occasionally nervous voices would penetrate the crushing silence, concern and tension evident in their words. I didn't listen, until I was able to open my eyes I wouldn't know if these people were with the Phoenix or not. Even then there was no guarantee they weren't holding me to sell me on to the highest bidder. Whatever happened, nothing was going to surprise me when I regained consciousness.

The next few days dragged slowly by as more and more of my senses returned to me. Occasionally the nervous voices were paired with blurry shadows which buzzed around my head and fiddled with machines and monitors whose beeps and whines became louder with every step back towards consciousness I took. On the final day of my journey back from my internal prison, my eyelids flickered open, focusing slowly as the dim strip light above my bed came into view. The cold, damp air hung about me, filling the grey-walled room with a musty scent which felt thick on my throat, as if I was trying to breathe in custard. Slowly I pushed myself up so that I was sitting. The room was windowless, with cracked plaster walls, showing the bricks beneath in places. One wall was covered in aged, yellow missing person posters. As I squinted at the faces which stared back at me without seeing it dawned on me that I had seen all these faces before. My foggy mind struggled with this for a while; I still wasn't fully up to speed, frustrated I flopped back onto the pillows, releasing a plume of dust which danced around my head in the beam of the neon light. Lazily I dozed back into a light sleep, even the sitting up and the quick examination of the posters on the wall had sapped a lot of my energy. I listened even though my eyes were closed, footsteps in the corridor caught my attention, and moments later the door creaked open on ancient hinges and the footsteps from outside began to make their way in. Cautiously I opened one eye, squinting at the tall, white coat clad figure who was studiously pouring over the notes and charts in a folder he had brought in with him. Nervously I coughed, breaking his concentration. He looked up at me from his notes, over his thin, silver framed spectacles, a smile dancing warmly at the corner of his brown eyes.

"Good, you're up," he began, voice serene and barely above a whisper.

"Yeah," I groaned, eyes open, "who is that good news for?"

"Well," he said, a bit more bite in his words, I'd offended him, "it's good news for you, first of all, living may be shit at times, but it can change, death is so final. It's good news for me, it means I've done a good enough job of reversing the effects of the kicking you took at the Queen Victoria hotel, and finally it's good news for her," he nodded to the door where a figure lurked behind the frosted glass, "she hasn't slept in a week, now you're up, maybe she'll get some rest."

I frowned, wincing as my bruised forehead contracted, "She, who is she?"

The doctor nodded at the door, which flew open almost instantaneously and in rushed a blur of purple hair, and black jumpsuit and worry. Adrienne flung her arms around my neck and crushed my throat with the biggest hug I'd ever had. "Dad," she sobbed into my neck, "I was so worried, John wouldn't let me go down from the balcony to help you I'm so sorry, I couldn't break out of his hold. I damn near killed him before the watchers burst in!"

I shrugged beneath the unmoving grasp. I patted her gently on the back, attempting to reassure her without words. The last time I'd seen Adrienne she had been ushered away from the unfolding beating by a huge man I had assumed was with the Joe and the Phoenix. The people who had smashed through the doors of the ballroom to rescue me must have been these "watchers" but I still had no idea who they were. All these questions spun around in my head, but I didn't vocalise them. Now wasn't the time, now I had to just be in the moment, being held by the daughter I thought I'd never see again, and embrace the fact that we were both safe and alive.

More time elapsed in silence between us. The only sound was the metronomic beep of the machine which counted the beats of my heart, unfaltering, unchanging, as their relentless procession continued. Eventually I sat up; Adrienne relinquished her constrictor grip on me enough for me to adjust my position. "I can't deny it, I did prefer the other place," I said.

She smiled, "Sorry Dad, that place was compromised when I took you there, the Alpha squad had to move out as soon as you left."

I shrugged, "Fair enough, I don't suppose you I could get out of here soon? The décor's not really up to much, and the artwork, well, the eyes follow me around the room."

Adrienne chuckled, "But Dad, you haven't moved since you got here; how do you know they follow you around the room?"

"They just look like they would," I mumbled in a painkiller induced daze.

She shrugged, "Well I suppose we can sort something out," she looked imploringly at the doctor, "what do you reckon Doc?"

The doctor looked up from his notes again, studied the heart rate monitor, looked at me, shrugged and said, "Well you're looking a lot better and your charts suggest that you're definitely on the mend, so I think you can get up and have a walk if you wish. Don't over exert yourself too much."

I smiled sarcastically, "Don't worry Doc, I'll try not to get shot, I guess that probably counts as over-exertion?"

He shrugged haughtily, yanking a little harder than was probably necessary to remove the IV line in my arm. The sarcasm hadn't gone down well with him. He trudged out, muttering angrily under his breath.

Adrienne watched him go before stepping off the bed and offering her hand to me. "Come on Dad, up you get."

I sighed, shrugged and began to meekly shuffle off the side of the bed. The bare concrete was cold on my feet, and putting weight through my legs for the first time in however long it had been made me wince. Adrienne's hand hovered over my shoulder, nervously watching my first unsteady steps as I stumbled towards the dressing gown which hung on the back of the door. Adrienne gave the room one final glance before following me into the corridor.

"So what is this place?" I began, looking up to the high, grey ceiling, illuminated with more neon strip lights.

"It's an abandoned factory, the Phoenix moved out of here when they found the hangar I rescued you from before," Adrienne replied, walking next to me, head bowed.

I nodded, I didn't want to know what they had been making here. Whatever it had been, it could have been one of the huge unknown undercover objects in the factory from my first tangle with the Phoenix. I stopped, the few steps along the corridor had begun to tire me, I turned to face Adrienne, "So, those people, at the ballroom, what happened?" I asked.

"Do you remember the emergency protocol code I showed you on the original ComChip?" she began, "well, Joe was the one who pushed for it, and in the new ComChip, that he announced at the ballroom," she hesitated, almost wary of my reaction before I had heard what she had to say, "it's not just for emergencies, as far as the public are concerned it's a necessary precaution, but Joe has complete control over the chip, and the people who have it implanted."

This new information echoed down the empty grey corridor as much as it had reverberated around in my head. I knew that Joe had been controlling the people in the ballroom; I had no idea how far-reaching the implications of the new ComChip could be, especially in the hands of a maniac.

"So," I began, slowly, the pieces of the puzzle falling together, "what exactly can Joe do to people who have the new chip implanted?" I looked up, studying Adrienne's face for clues as to what was going to be said next.

She sighed heavily, staring intently at her feet, "Anything, I suppose, the new chip isn't in the hand like the prototype. It's implanted into the back of the neck to give easier access to the neuro relays and brain stem. In theory it could be used to gain information about a person, or, in the case of the people in the ballroom, switch off the ability to think for themselves and give the controller what is, in effect, a puppet army. That was a small test. We've heard that soon the Phoenix are planning to release it worldwide."

I swallowed the lump in my throat that had been rising steadily as Adrienne had been speaking, I wasn't sure if it was because of the mixture of painkillers swimming through my system or what she was saying, but the lump had risen in my throat, shortening my breaths and making it hard to concentrate on what I'd been told. One question kept forcing its way to the front of my mind, it made its way out of my mouth before I had a chance to stop it. "Ok, so where do you and the Alpha squad come into this?" I nodded down the corridor at the two guards on stools outside other rooms, their distance obscuring their features.

"We're the reason that the Phoenix hasn't been able to launch a series of attacks on the world so far, a group of double agents who found out about what was going on within the organisation and decided to try and put a stop to it." The pride swelled in her chest. "How are we doing Dad?" she smiled, for the first time almost fishing for my approval.

I smiled back at her, "I couldn't be more proud," I said, "do you have any idea what Joe is planning?"

Her smile vanished as quickly as it had come. “I’m sorry Dad, I don’t, the Phoenix have been quiet recently, we haven’t been able to infiltrate the highest levels since the hangar escapade and having lost Mark and Mum–” her voice trailed off, a tear had formed in the corner of her eye, she brushed it away, looking back from the floor into my eyes, lip beginning to quiver.

Instinctively I reached out, wrapping an arm around her. “You have done brilliantly so far,” I said, “and your Mother, I didn’t know she was part of it. I can’t even say that I remember her, but we can finish this, together, for her, for Mark, for all of them.”

She straightened up, gathered her resolve and cleared her throat. “Absolutely.” I could see the fire had returned to her, the desire and drive to fight for what she believed in, the one thing I had always hoped any child of mine would possess. We smiled at each other, the silent pact had been agreed, and we were both in this until the end; whatever the end would be.

Chapter Seventeen

Over the next few days more of my strength returned to me, until one day I was able to walk all the way from my corridor to the main work room. Adrienne stood poring over a chart which had been spread over a table in the centre of the room. Two large screens illuminated the room, one scrolling through numbers, almost too fast to recognise, the other used the first to plot co-ordinates on a slowly rotating globe. There were plenty of other people in the room, buzzing from room to room, carrying armfuls of weapons, papers and boxes. There was an instant difference between these people and the drones which had been labouring under Joe. They looked like they wanted to be here, driven and united by the cause. Adrienne looked up from the chart spread across the table as my footsteps echoed into the cavernous hall. "Dad, you're up," she beamed, half running through the crowd of people toward me, "what do you think?" She gestured to the screens and activity that was going on all around us.

I glanced around, the energy in the room was phenomenal, an almost tangible belief which leapt from person to person, binding them together. "It's great," I smiled, "do they all work for you?" Adrienne looked around, smiled, and nodded, "Yeah Dad, we recruited a lot of people from the lower levels of the Phoenix, often before they had the ComChip implanted, which made it easier to keep them from becoming susceptible to psychological intrusions."

"Psychological intrusions, like the numbers in my head?" I said.

"Exactly that," Adrienne said, "although we're not sure why the override code was given to you, as soon as you tried to remove your chip we managed to intercept it," she waved at the screen of numbers, "we managed to use the intercepted transmission and use the override to free a lot of innocents who had bought the original in good faith that it was going to be used for communication only."

I rubbed my chin, almost ruefully, those people had been exposed to Joe's world through no fault of their own; some of them could have done terrible things without knowing, all because of me. The lost and broken lives of countless people on my conscience burned in the pit of my stomach, I refused to be responsible for any more, the Phoenix had to be taken down. Once and for all. "So if you managed to decipher the original ComChip security code, and free all those people, what is that doing now?" I pointed up to the constantly scrolling numbers. Almost immediately, before Adrienne had a chance to answer, the answer leapt across a synapse, "Of course, the whole reason they launched the second version of the ComChip was because they had found out the prototype had been hacked, so they must have re-designed the second one to be far harder to access! You're trying to hack the new version!" I spun breathless with excitement to face Adrienne, who stood there, as if she hadn't expected me to figure it out so quickly, a look of shock and pride spreading over her face. Pieces of the puzzle were beginning to fit together as if someone had flicked a switch in my head, a sudden rush of adrenaline sparked the life back into me, a rush that not even nicotine or drunkenness had ever come close to. Colours seemed far more vivid, the humming of the electric appliances all around us seemed somehow louder, almost as if I was suddenly back on the frequency of the world, connected to everything around me. After having been lost in a haze of cigarette smoke, alcohol and depression, it felt as though the mist had cleared, leaving me able to function on a level I had not experienced in what felt like forever.

This new-found determination forced me forward, up the steps onto the plinth where the two screens were mounted. I darted between them, frantically searching for the connection between the continually changing numbers and the slowly rotating globe. "Come on, come on, come on." I murmured hastily under my breath, tapping quickly at my temples in an attempt to fire my brain back up, to match the energy that coursed through me. "What am I missing here?" I muttered, "there's something blindingly obvious I can't see here." I turned to look back at Adrienne and the gaggle of white-coated scientists who had all stopped what they were doing to watch my frantic ramblings. My paces were interrupted by the doctor, who stepped out from behind one of the consoles and placed his hand gently on my shoulder. "It's ok, Michael," he said, the reassuring tone of his voice soothing the pounding in my ears, "you've been out of this a long time, take it easy, small steps, ok?"

I looked up into his kind face, the gentle smile played in his eyes, calming me still further from the heated adrenaline flush which had been controlling my movements and thoughts up until now. I shrugged his hand off and turned back to the screens, "Do you think Joe is resting? Taking small steps?" I grumbled, as more red dots appeared on the globe.

The doctor stepped around me, blocking my view to the screen and stared hard into my face. "Joe doesn't know you're back, that helps us. It means we can launch a raid on the Phoenix's science and technology division sooner than he would have anticipated, but as long as he doesn't know you've regained a lot of the mental functions the coma and subsequent depression took from you, we have time to retrain your mind, get you back completely, without a rush. We can keep Joe distracted for a while. Those red dots," he waved at the globe behind him, "are us, we're infiltrating and sabotaging these locations, which are factories or laboratories, we're delaying the release of the ComChip 2 to the public. This means that Joe is busy enough at the minute, he's plugging leaks rather than coming after us."

I chuckled quietly to myself; musing on the idea of Joe's control room being inundated with red-faced interns reluctantly relaying the news that yet another of their factories or labs had been damaged or destroyed gave me an immense amount of pleasure. I imagined the calm exterior had been distinctly ruffled and the glimmer of malice in his green eyes had been replaced by cold dread as he had to straighten his tie, stand a little taller, take a large, reluctant breath and walk into a room of his superiors to explain why no progress was being made.

Chapter Eighteen

Unseen by all of us near the screens, a guard at the back of the room shifted nervously from foot to foot, checking his phone, finally, he took one last look at it, before he lifted his machine gun and charged forward, firing a continuous stream of bullets into the four guards behind Adrienne. I turned just to see his crazed eyes before the doctor threw himself on top of me and pushed me to the ground. A couple of wayward bullets flew over our heads and smashed into the screens which sparked and hummed as the circuitry inside them was shredded. More bullets flew through the air, hitting the first two who fell with an agonised yelp, as the bullets thudded into their backs, the other two spun around as their colleagues fell, pulling Adrienne to the floor and returning fire on the lone assailant. His wayward firing was soon brought to a halt as the two guards emptied entire magazines into his chest, the first few bullets stopping him in his tracks, the remainder tearing bloody holes in his head and torso before he fell gracelessly back into a pool of his own blood, which spread out from underneath him.

The angry clatter of bullets died immediately, the sudden silence hitting harder than I could've expected. I hadn't been shot at for at least a week, so the shock of someone firing a gun in my direction had returned. The smoke cleared, allowing us all the time to take in what had just happened, the guards' bodies were hastily pulled clear of the room by tentative guards who had come running from the corridors when they heard the melee ensue.

Adrienne reacted first as I was still reeling from the shock. She stood back up and began barking orders at guards, "Lock this place down! No-one gets in or out until we know who he was and how much he knew." She turned from the guards to me. "Are you OK Dad?" she asked, a hurried tension in her voice.

I waved my arms and patted down my front, "I'm fine," I smiled weakly, "all in a day's work."

She nodded, "Good, you need to leave here, go with the doctor to the safe house, I'll meet you there when we've got everything back under control." She hugged me quickly then sprinted back to the guards who were busy pulling down large metal shutters to close the doors.

"Come on," the doctor's voice pulled me out of the daze I had been in. "We have to go." He escorted me firmly away, his hand surprisingly strong on my shoulder. I nodded, still shocked. I took one final look around the room, watching Adrienne busy herself with assisting the guards in shoring up the cavernous room's defences. I turned slowly and followed him away behind one of the screens and down a hatch to a dark and narrow tunnel with pipes that whistled and hissed in the dark by my ears. The doctor clicked on a torch ahead of me, illuminating the dark, black walled passage which was barely wide enough for me to squeeze down. "Where are we–" I began.

"Not here," the doctor whispered hurriedly, "wait until we're out of here, we're still in danger here." He continued to stump forward waving his torch at the sides of the tunnel, the dark walls which stretched out away beyond the reach of the torchlight. We continued forward into the darkness, the only sound penetrating the silence between us was the hissing and spitting of the steam which burst from the holes in the ancient pipes. Occasionally, we passed a large metal grate which threw a small amount of light into the musty passage. I paused at one, looking into the wide, open room, which had been abandoned by Joe and his men, in, by the looks of it, a hurry, tables were overturned, papers had been torn off the walls and there were scorch marks spreading along the floor from the centre of the room and up the walls, as if the entire room had been doused in petrol and left to burn.

As the questions began to float their way to the surface of my mind, the doctor returned back from ahead of me to pull me onward. "We can't stop Michael," he whispered, "we have to reach the safe house, quickly." He pushed his hand onto my back and forced me forward into the dark ahead of him. Forward again we hurried; the echoes of our footsteps were curtailed by the narrowness of the corridor we had been trudging along for what seemed like days. "How long have we been walking?" I moaned. Although I had been recovering well, the high of the adrenaline had been steadily ebbing away the further we had moved away from the room I had left Adrienne barricading in preparation for the upcoming battle of which I guessed the lone gunman was solely a precursor. "Not long," the doctor replied shortly, "about three hours."

I sighed heavily, with each step my legs ached more, three hours, it felt more like three damn years. I said as much to the doctor, who chuckled under his breath, handed me a bottle of water and instructed me to take it easy, as it was the only water we had until we arrived at the safe house. I thirstily slurped from the bottle as the refreshing clear liquid crashed past my cracked and dry lips. As I removed the bottle from my mouth I sighed in rejuvenated satisfaction, replaced the lid and handed it back to the doctor. "Cheers," I whispered.

"No problem," he replied, "now, do you think we can get to the safe house without any more of your bitching?"

I chuckled; his tone was more jovial than the cutting remark suggested. I guessed it was his revenge for how bad a patient I had been during my recovery. "Yeah, I reckon so," I smiled in the darkness, "I'm an old man though, bitching is what I do."

He laughed behind me, jokingly pushing me in the back, "Come on then grandpa, let's get to the safe house."

Three further hours passed, I assumed it had been three hours as it dragged by as much as the first three. The doctor reached out and placed his hand on my shoulder. "Ok Michael," he squeezed gently to bring me to a halt, "we're here."

Chapter Nineteen

The torchlight over my shoulder illuminated a door to the left of me, a small, glowing panel with a numeric keypad beneath it protruding at my waist height. The doctor pushed past me and stooped at the panel. As he finished prodding at the keys, the door slid aside with a hiss to reveal a small, bright white lift, just big enough for the doctor and me to stand inside. The short journey upwards gave my eyes time to adjust to the light that streamed from the bulbs above our heads. A second hiss of the doors signalled our arrival at the safe house. The doctor strode out of the lift and down the dark, damp, old corridor towards the light of the doorway to a room to the left. Before he entered, he turned back to look down the corridor to me, "Come on Michael, your dinner's getting cold." My rumbling stomach overruled my fear of what could be out there, away from the relative safety of the lift. Tentatively, I stepped forward, padding down the richly carpeted corridor, the smell of the food behind the kitchen door wafting temptingly toward me.

The kitchen was bright, airy but old-fashioned; a huge range took up almost the whole of one wall, with a large chimney breast protruding from behind it. The pans and crockery lined up along shelves on another wall, glittering in the lights which hung down from the ceiling above the sparse table, with its plain wood and two steaming plates, piled high with bacon, sausages, eggs, baked beans and toast. My stomach gave another, louder rumble before I hurriedly fell upon the food, shovelling the hot food into my mouth and enjoying the warm sensation the mixture of fried meat and bread gave as they slid down my throat, satisfying the hunger that had gnawed in my guts all the way along the escape tunnels.

The doctor set his knife and fork down with a clatter and leant back, placing a satisfied hand on his distended stomach, patting it gently before leaning across the table, hands folded. "I'm guessing you have a few questions," he said.

I chewed the mouthful of soft yellow egg yolks and chewy, salty bacon quicker in order to swallow and answer his question. "Yeah, just a few," I murmured quickly, taking a replenishing drink from the large mug of tea that had been set on the table next to me. "Who was the guard? Why did he open fire on us, and why did we come here?" The three questions tumbled out of my mouth before I could sequence them or slowly ask. The doctor smiled, as the barrage of questions sank in.

He took a deep breath, exhaled slowly and began to answer my flurry of questions, "The guard was one of Joe's berserkers, just as we've infiltrated the Phoenix, they've infiltrated us too; it's harder for them, because we are a smaller organisation, so there are fewer faces we don't know. But occasionally, they get past us, and we have to lockdown the base we're at after an attack like that."

"So it's happened before?" A pang of fear struck in my newly-filled gut, Adrienne had been running away from these 'berserkers' most of the years I'd been gone.

The doctor shrugged. “Only a couple of times,” he smiled, “we’ve had a tighter grip on our security, and when it happens we lock the place down and move on before anyone from the Phoenix can catch us.”

I nodded, reassured. The doctor’s calm words soothed my nervousness and allowed me to focus on what the doctor was telling me, instead of panicking in my head and being distracted by those thoughts.

The doctor drummed his fingers on the table before pointing at me. “You’ve met some of these berserkers before.”

I cocked my head to the right, frowning slightly, struggling with memories of possible encounters with these ‘berserkers’. It dawned on me slowly. “The ballroom,” I muttered under my breath.

The doctor nodded. He looked relieved that there was no need to dredge it up too much for me to remember. All the pieces fell together, slowly at first, but as more and more pieces began to slide together the picture grew faster and faster. Again I felt the burning adrenaline begin to spark up my brain, “The override code was never for safety,” I whispered excitedly. “Joe put it there so he could toy with their minds, he could do anything, take their bank details, sexual fantasies, political persuasions, or even turn them into mindless soldiers.” I had known this already, but now I could see the bigger picture, how the Phoenix could take over the world, keep the people subdued and eradicate anyone who got too close to the truth. Joe was only a pawn in his own chess game, the puppeteer was the puppet. I smiled again, slowly, wondering if Joe even knew that his superiors regarded him in the same way as he regarded the rest of the world, expendable.

Calmed by the realisation that Joe's position was as precarious as ours I continued with my questioning, "So what is this place?" I gestured at the kitchen around us, the tiled floor grimy on closer inspection.

"We're here because this was the last safe house on the list we had," the doctor replied, "after this, we're out of places to hide."

I sighed resignedly, "We have to stand and fight then. No more running."

The doctor nodded grimly. "No more running," he echoed in stout agreement.

Chapter Twenty

I didn't sleep that night, the bed was cold and hard, inside the thin and musty sheets I turned and twisted uncomfortably, unable to find a position that accommodated and comforted my body against the ancient springs. About half past five in the morning, as the first rays of sunlight began to push their way past the thin curtains and mucky windows to caress my cheek, a sharp rap on the door brought me out of the stupor I had found myself in. I heard the doctor shuffle out of his room and down the stairs to the front door. There was a slight silent pause before a chain was slipped loose and locks were clicked open. A muffled voice quietly and hastily conveyed a message to the doctor, and, although I couldn't make out the words, the general tone of the conversation was panicked and downcast.

A few minutes later, the door swung shut again, the chain slid back on and the locks were secured. The doctor sighed heavily, before slowly making his way back up the stairs again. Two hours later he knocked on my door, quietly at first, but louder on the second and third attempts. I had heard the first two, but didn't want to hear the news I was bound to be given when I allowed the doctor into my room. The two extra knocks gave me the time to collect my thoughts and sit up slowly on the firm pillows. After the third knock I answered, "Come in!" My voice took me by surprise. A lot of dust must have landed on my face, collecting in my nose and throat, which gave it a groggy, sore sound.

The doctor's face crept around the corner of my door and peered in at me, sitting in my bed. "Good Michael, you're up," he said, slowly, picking his next words carefully. He ventured into the room, presenting me with a huge mug of tea and a plate of toast, which he placed down on the bedside table before standing back a few paces to allow me space in my room. "Look Michael," he stammered over the words, "we had some news during the night, and it wasn't good I'm afraid." He stared at me, assessing me for my reaction. Even though I had been fully awake for two hours the fog of drowsiness still hung over me.

I nodded; a sneaking sense of dread began to creep into my lower abdomen. "Go on," I prompted, "what was this news?" I waited with baited breath as the doctor rocked back and forth on his toes, fumbling over the words, struggling to put the sentence together.

"Last night," he began, slowly, taking deep breaths and a long time between each word, "the factory we had been holed up in was attacked. A small squad of Phoenix soldiers broke past the main gates, tore down the fences and charged the building." He stopped, squinting at me, trying to read my expression.

"Go on," I nodded again, prompting him imploringly, neither of us wanting to hear the words that I felt coming.

He took one last shuddering breath before imparting the worst part of the news. "Adrienne was taken, we haven't heard anything about whether or not she was alive, but the rest of the squad at the factory were gunned down."

I swung my legs over the side of the bed and put my head in my hands, the tears burning in my dusty eyes, the raging tumult of fear and anger swept over me, all encompassing, it made it impossible to think clearly, as if a swarm of wasps had been agitated into buzzing around my skull by the doctor's words. I looked up from the cradle of my hands into the doctor's anguished face. The words tumbled from my numb lips, "We have to get her back."

The doctor leant forward to place a reassuring hand on my shoulder and nodded in solemn agreement, "We will," he muttered from behind gritted teeth, it was strange, his voice was strained; as if he was biting back tears. "We will."

The day passed agonisingly slowly, the doctor flitted in and out of the house, often talking on his phone as he headed down the street, I watched him go, his figure flicking past the window behind the net curtain. I sat on the ancient leather sofa, staring at the opposite wall, its old, yellowed and peeling wallpaper held my attention. I wasn't really staring at the wall itself, it was just where my eyes had rested as torturous images danced in my mind. Adrienne's screaming as the electrodes which had dispatched Mark so viciously sent their burning current through her writhing body. Mark, Katherine, the berserker in the factory, the berserkers in the ballroom, all these images played out on a constant loop; I shook my head vigorously, trying to remove the gruesome pictures from my mind to no avail. I stood up from the sofa slowly; the leather and wood creaked with relief as I vacated it. I wasn't heavy, especially not after my recent imprisonment at the hands of Joe or my later stay in hospital, but the sofa was so old and worn, that the wood creaked with an arthritic groan each time I moved on the cracked red leather. I wandered from one room to another, my attention caught by a large black book and pen on the kitchen table. I slid out a chair from under the table and sat, running my hands over the smooth cover before opening it. The pages were blank lined paper, apart from a note at the top of the first one, "Write it out." The doctor's casual scrawl had predicted that I would need somewhere to store the thoughts that hummed in my head. The wasps in my mind were quieter that day, a mere hum of background noise. I began to write, diarising the events that had happened so far, drawing out the venom of the wasp stings, soothing the buzzing sound in my ears. The pen danced over the paper, almost without thought or guidance, spidery letters weaving words which covered the first three pages in what felt like no time at all. I looked back over my morning's work, annotated it, with added thoughts that came to mind on the second reading.

By the time I had finished looking over my notes and scribbling the doctor returned, head bowed as he shuffled into the kitchen. "Good, you found it," he said, waving a hand half-heartedly at the book which I had closed as he came in.

I nodded, "Yeah, thanks, it's been helpful." He smiled, that was obviously a relief to him, after what I thought could not have been a good morning, "Any more news?" I quizzed, the nerves twisting in my guts as the wasps began to buzz louder in my head.

The doctor moved from the doorway of the kitchen to the table. He took a chair from the other side of the table and placed his hands carefully in front of himself, clasping them within one another. He took a deep breath, shook his head and started, “No, none of Adrienne,” he murmured, once again, the tears swimming in his eyes. “But we have to move from here, reports are coming in that Joe’s raiding party is searching all the passages and rooms leading out of the factory, eventually, they’ll find the one we came down, and find us here. They may be on their way already.”

The nerves hadn’t been abated by the news the doctor had imparted. I stood up, the background buzzing in my head growing steadily louder as more questions bubbled to the surface. “So what do we do?” I asked hastily. I paced the grimy kitchen floor three paces forward and three back, my breaths shorter and shallower as the fear rose in my throat.

“We leave.” The short syllables bit back, almost too short an answer.

I understood, every minute we spent talking about the possible escapes the boots crunched down the corridors we had scurried down the day before. I grabbed the book and pen off the table, and headed to the hallway. I hadn’t brought any other possessions with me so the clearing up of the house took less than twenty minutes. The doctor gave the house one final sweep to ensure we hadn’t left anything behind, before he handed me a thick black coat with a hood, and gestured towards the door. “Off we go.”

The cold wind of autumn bit hard as we stepped out into the street, I shuddered, and pulled the hood over my ears. The doctor followed me out, locked the door with a string of keys which he slipped back into his pocket. “Come on,” he nodded down the street to the left, as I had begun to walk off to the right. I spun on my heels and followed him silently, too concerned that there were too many eyes out here to ask where we were going. I already knew that the Alpha squad was already out of hiding places, so wherever we were going it wasn't going to be safe. That didn't matter too much to me, as wherever Adrienne was being held definitely wasn't anywhere near as safe.

Adrienne. As I thought of my daughter the image of her screaming face swam before my open eyes, it was a punch in the gut that stopped me, only momentarily. The doctor heard my faltering footsteps, and turned back to face me. I looked up to him, studying his face more closely than I had done before. His face was young, younger than I thought he had been on first sight, closer to Adrienne's age than mine. I suddenly understood his tears as much as mine; he was in love with my daughter. "What's your name, Doc?" I asked with a new-found connection to him.

He smiled, "Just call me Doc, everyone does."

I grinned, "I will, but if you want to be with my daughter, I'd prefer to know your name at least once." I gently pushed him for an answer as I straightened up and continued down the street.

He stumbled in his shock for a moment, "How did you–"

I looked into his brown eyes and chuckled, "It's obvious really, each time you've mentioned her since she's been captured you've been struggling not to cry." I patted him on the back, "You're a good guy, and I give you permission to date my purple-haired assassin daughter when this is all over, as I'm pretty sure you're not going to leave her and, even if you did, I think she could deal with you a lot better than I could."

He laughed nervously, smiling back at me, "My name is Doctor Jason Cole." A weight seemed to lift from his shoulders, as the relief flooded into his eyes.

“Nice to meet you, Doc.” I laughed, before continuing forward.

Doc’s footsteps seemed slightly brighter after our little conversation, as we walked into a bus station. The old concrete was chipped and cracking beneath the grim strip lights which cast a yellow light down upon the few people sitting on the metal benches, their eyes empty and cold, it was as if we had stepped into the end of the world. Everyone there looked devoid of hope, all waiting for their respective buses and coaches to carry them away from whatever had left them here and desolate in the first place. I sat on one of the benches towards the back of the station, away in a corner, the metal rang as I flopped down on it, my legs ached from the walk, no matter how much better I had been feeling lately, I was still recovering from the recent coma and, as Doc had left the stash of painkillers he had managed to sneak out of the factory on our escape behind, my strength was beginning to wane again. Doc came to sit down beside me, the tickets he had just bought clutched in his hands.

“Where are we going?” I whispered under my breath, nodding slightly at the tickets.

Doc looked down to his hands. “Somewhere further up north,” he whispered, “can’t say too much now, too many ears.” He flicked the tickets in his hands at the gaunt ghosts that kept us company haunting the station. I grunted quietly in agreement, I knew that Joe and the Phoenix could be listening, even though he wasn’t personally within earshot. Time edged by painfully slowly, coaches pulled in and one by one, the ghosts vacated the station until four hours had passed and Doc and I were the only ones remaining.

Chapter Twenty-One

Eventually, our coach lumbered into the station. The neon lights played on the dirty white paint as the coach came to a gradual halt. The hum of the engine became louder as Doc and I approached the behemoth that would carry us away from the eerie station which felt haunted, as if the souls of the people who had left hours before had been marooned here to wander the cold floors for all eternity. Doc waved the tickets at the driver, who nodded slowly and waved us down the coach. Doc found two seats toward the back and flopped down, giving a sigh of relief as the cushioned seat welcomed his tired back. I followed and squirmed in comfort as the tiredness flowed through me. "I'm going to get some sleep," I muttered to Doc, who nodded quietly, before retrieving a small, matte black Walther P99 from an inside coat pocket. He slid a magazine into the handle and secreted it beneath his coat. It took me aback slightly, that even here, on an empty coach, Doc felt the need to be armed, just how dangerous this world actually was hit me hard. Adrienne's anguished face swam behind my eyelids again, the terror twisted in my stomach. I felt trapped here, on the coach which was pulling away from the station, with no idea where I was going, if it was going to bring me closer to saving my daughter from the clutches of the Phoenix.

I slept fitfully. The vibrations of the engine soothed my nerves, but only slightly. When I awoke up I didn't feel rested. My shoulders ached with the tension I had been carrying and the buzz of the wasps in my head returned even louder than before. The book Doc had given me was cradled in my arms; I placed it on my lap and opened it to a blank page. I stared at it for what felt like an age, the buzz of the wasps louder, just below a dull roar; the focus I needed to plan in order to save Adrienne wasn't forthcoming. I held the pen to the paper and watched the ink spread out from the nib in a rounded pool which reminded me of the blood that had spread from mk. 2's body after Adrienne had shot him. I had seen too much blood since this had started, Katherine's, the blue-eyed man's, mk.2's and my own. The anger began to course through me as I sat, rigid with fury at what the Utopian dreams I had once harboured had become in the hands of Joe and the Phoenix.

The blue-eyed man's face leapt into my mind out of nowhere, how did he tie into this entangled web of violence and deception? I knew I couldn't think of that now, Adrienne's plight was my priority and I had to keep the distractions and permutations of my actions out of my head for the moment. As Doc had said, small steps.

The miles of grey tarmac surrounded by rolling fields gave way to the eventual city destination of the coach as the light began to fade from the day. The streets were narrower with tall buildings crowding over our route as the bus pulled into another station, 'another holding cell for the journeymen', I thought as we arrived. We left quickly via a side exit, a dark, cavernous tunnel with flickering lights, crackling behind the yellowed plastic which had filled up with the corpses of insects unlucky enough to find their way in and never make it out again. One or two were trying to fight their way out; they flew fruitlessly headlong into the unmoved, aged plastic coffin that was to become their final resting place. Their struggle struck a chord with me, seeing their predecessors die around them and doing everything they could to avoid it, with no success. I had a sneaking sympathy with them. Every move they were making was being scrutinised by me, as I'm sure Joe was scrutinising every move I made. It wouldn't be necessary to use observers through the ComChip, as I had learned from Doc on the journey that the Phoenix controlled the majority of the CCTV network in the country.

My attention was drawn from the insect's battle against their plastic prison to the corner of the corridor we were standing in, the red light blinked under the rectangular camera which protruded from the wall. As I stared at it the lens moved ever so gradually to meet my gaze. I stared furiously at it, willing my silent anger to translate through the camera to the room of screens, in the hope that Joe could see me. I knew it was unlikely and all it would do would alert him and the Phoenix to where Doc and I were, but I didn't care. He had to see that he hadn't broken me, that I was still standing; and I was coming to save my daughter and reduce his entire empire to ashes.

Doc's rough grab pulled me out of my inanimacy, he shook me vigorously out of my silent rage. "What are you doing?" he bellowed, his angry voice echoing down the corridor. Fuming, he pulled my hood back over my head, turned me away from the camera's unwavering stare and pushed me away towards the cool night air. It hit me like a wall, the dense, piss-stained air was replaced instantly by a cold breeze which swept the descending red cloud from my mind. Doc shoved me forcefully into it from the undercover safety of the tunnel. "I told you they had control of the CCTV and that's what you do?" Doc fumed in front of me. "Why not just hang a fucking great neon sign around your neck saying, 'Here I am, come and get me!'?" I stood in front of him, my head hung silently, as if I was being chastised by a favourite uncle.

"I'm sorry," I mumbled.

"You're sorry, that's great, just great Michael. Will your sorry get us the element of surprise back? Will it help us get closer to Adrienne?" His voice cracked with impassioned strain as he said her name. He gritted his teeth and continued, "Come on, we have to get off the streets, the sooner the better." Without another word he turned on his heels, and broke into long strides, I had to jog to catch up with him.

The buildings in this part of town had been abandoned for what looked like years. Cracked or missing windows stared, unseeing like empty eye-sockets. Graffiti-covered bricks and charred marks riddled the boards covering the entrances where people had stubbed out hundreds of cigarettes in the time the buildings had stood abandoned. I felt comfortable amongst the broken buildings; since this battle with Joe and the Phoenix had begun I had felt increasingly as though the pristine world held no place for me, I had been ostracised and feared by anyone who had seen my face. The scars the guards had given me in my first encounter with Joe's men at the secret laboratory had been etched into my skin, in the same way someone may carve their initials into the bark of a tree. It was noticeable in the street, with people in their clean suits and ties slowing to look at me before scurrying away. Some of them had glowing hands from the first ComChip or some even had a nick on the back of their necks to denote they had the second version of the ComChip implanted. Here though, amongst the burned out buildings, no-one looked twice at an aged man, dirty, with a straggly beard and scars, the anonymity felt like a warm embrace. 'Finally,' I thought, 'I match my surroundings.'

A little way ahead, Doc had stopped at a building, rapping sharply on the wooden covering, two short knocks followed by an open hand slap on the door. The hinged piece of thin wood swung outward to reveal a two inch thick steel plate which had been bolted to the wood, unseen from the outside. A cautious female face poked out from the gap it had vacated. She beckoned us inside. Doc stepped in confidently, motioning for me to join them. I took a final deep breath of the city's cool night air to settle the squirming nerves in the pit of my stomach and followed him inside.

Chapter Twenty-Two

The corridor behind the door was not much wider than me, but at least two feet taller, with pipes hissing in the darkness above our heads as we followed our host down the tunnel as it twisted further into the bowels of the building. Eventually, we reached a cavernous room, and it became obvious that the hideout we had been invited into had at one stage been a shopping centre. Dried fountains and pools stood forlornly at the corners of the main concourse, cracked televisions hung from the ceiling, occasionally sparking into life, crackling as the grey and black streaks of static danced across the screen, then fading as quickly as they had started up. The ceiling tiles had been removed to expose the skeletal framework of pipes and wires which clung to the concrete ceiling like the veins and arteries of a vast sprawling corpse, once carrying the life-blood of this gargantuan structure, alive and humming with activity, but now silent and defunct. Old oil drums were dotted sporadically between the pillars; the flames within them crackled merrily, throwing wavy shadows onto the metal shutters of the abandoned shop fronts.

Slowly, more cautious faces began to appear from the shadows, all of them wearing the same black hoods as the people at the ballroom. A knot began to tie itself in my stomach, tighter with every step that the hooded mass took. I looked at Doc, who had found a man propped up against one of the sturdy pillars with a nasty cut to his head. A quiet murmur began to sweep through the ever-increasing crowd; some of them had removed their hoods to stare at me, as though seeing me had completely defied any belief.

One stepped forward from the crowd, removing the hood as she strode toward me. The curiosity fear and tiredness mixed in her eyes made her look older, but I guessed she couldn't be more than thirty-five. "M-M-Mr Wolf?" she said, her voice trembling just above a whisper.

I smiled back at her, "That's me," I said, still trying to figure out who these people were, why Doc had brought me here, and how any of this was going to help me get back to Adrienne.

The shocked relief overcame the woman in front of me, she lurched forward, throwing her arms around my neck and hugging me tightly. "It's so good to see you!" she grinned broadly, displaying perfectly white teeth. "We were told you were dead, some of the protest swore they pulled you out of the ballroom, but Doc hadn't been able to tell us anything over the phone, just that he was coming here with a visitor."

I nodded, "So you guys are the ones that pulled me out of that beating, I guess I should thank you, without you all I'd be dead." I looked to the crowd behind the woman, an increasing number of faces visible as hoods were removed. They were a complete mixture of people, all ages, races and genders, all with the same, sad, sorry look in their eyes, as if they had been watching the televisions for news, only to never hear what they wanted to hear.

She smiled back at me, even more broadly than before. "You're more than welcome, Mr Wolf," she said, "without you, our last hope for answers would've died." She stopped, to stare at me, as if calculating her next move.

"Well," I said slowly, "I was hoping you could give me some answers." I stared back into her clear blue eyes, "Who are you for a start?"

Her smile faded for a moment, "We're the faceless, Mr Wolf, the protestors against the Phoenix and its ever closer involvement with government. We were set up because we have all lost relatives to the Phoenix; they went to work and never came back, or just disappeared after buying Phoenix tech. Our founders had discovered the secrets of what the Phoenix has in store." She broke off again, eyes wide with fear, "I can't say too much more, just know this; you thought things are bad now. They're about to get a whole lot worse."

Her words sank in like an icy dagger, I didn't know how much worse things could get, but the fear in the room had spread like a pool of tar, slowly sticking to the people around us, making them tense up and shudder. 'Fuck,' I thought, 'just one more reason to take down these bastards before the Faceless' predicted shitstorm hits.'

"I hate to interrupt this touching moment," a familiar voice boomed. "But now you're all together, we can begin. You're live on Phoenix TV, please do not swear."

'Too late. Shitstorm's hit land.'

There was suddenly a lot more light in the cavernous concourse, one of the television screens had burst into life, and there, smugly sat in a high backed chair, hands folded, staring down at us, was Joe. The hoods returned swiftly to their owner's heads and most of them scuttled back into the darkness like cockroaches avoiding the light.

Joe chuckled as he watched them flee. "Now then," he began, "I know that some of you 'Faceless' are just not as involved with the movement as others; in a moment, a shutter will open and you will be able to walk out of here without any recourse." He paused. To the right hand side of the television, the metal shutter juddered into life, screeching upwards to allow people to walk into a dark department store which stood silently, like the jaws of a terrifying creature of the deep. Everything inside me screamed for no-one to move, to hope that the people I was with weren't stupid enough to believe that Joe would just let them walk out of here. Initially no-one moved; after a while a voice from the shadows called out, "I'm sorry Jeanette, I have to go, I have to." A woman scurried across the cracked tiles, looked back apologetically at the woman and me standing before the television, and stepped into the store. Three more people followed suit, all apologetic and timid as they backed away. More people followed them, convinced that nothing would happen to them if they fled. By the end of the exodus only a handful of the Faceless remained. Joe nodded, "Very well," he said, pressing a button on the arm of his chair. The shutter slammed down with a force that echoed down the corridors from the main hall. It was only the shutter closing but for me, it felt like the clang of a guillotine.

Gunfire rattled through the store, flashes of light exploding from the ends of machine guns which had been secreted in the aisles of the store. The screams of outrage at the betrayal and terror at the inevitable fate they faced rose to a cacophony as bodies danced through a hail of bullets; their shadows painting a macabre shadow-puppetry show onto the walls of the shopping centre. The last few to enter the store tried to scramble free, punching and scraping on the metal shutter in a vain attempt to make it move. A final thunderous round of gunfire silenced them.

The iron of the blood from the fresh corpses mingled with the lingering smoke from the barrels of the machine guns and poured through the holes in the metal shutter and wafted languorously across the hall to where Jeanette, Doc and I were standing motionless. Jeanette had buried her face into my chest and was sobbing quietly at the thought of her fallen comrades. I stood still, allowing the bloody scent to wash over me, fuelling me for the next onslaught that Joe had planned.

His voice floated from the screen above us over the shaking sobs of Jeanette. I raised my head to stare at the cold, merciless green eyes.

"You evil son of a bitch," I spat, my burning stare unwaveringly meeting his.

He smiled, the cold malice never leaving his eyes. "You knew it was going to happen," he shrugged, "they were an inconvenience, one my employers had been able to tolerate or use to our advantage up until this point. They had outlived their purpose and needed to be," he paused over the last word, running his tongue over his teeth, "eliminated."

Jeanette's shuddering sobs became louder as Joe's voice faded away. I rubbed her back, eyes not moving from the screen. "I knew you were a soulless bastard, but these people, they were completely innocent, they just wanted to find closure."

Joe chuckled, “And now they have,” a mock cajoling tone in his voice. “Now, if you’ll excuse me, I believe there’s about to be a news conference you’ll want to see.”

He pushed a button on his desk and the screen changed to a press conference. Regal flags draped down behind the podium and microphones protruded up from the top as if they were antennae. A bumbling, shabby figure in a suit which was too small for him shuffled onto the podium, his sweaty brow and fat jowls sat perched on the collar which disappeared beneath his second chin. He straightened the papers which had been placed in front of him by a nervous intern who backed away out of shot. An introductory banner slid across the bottom of the screen, announcing the man behind the podium as the Prime Minister. I stood there, in the abandoned shopping centre, Jeanette’s sobs still echoing up to the cavernous ceiling. I felt fear from what I was watching; it made me shake internally in time with every pounding thump of my heart, even though I was standing still.

The Prime Minister’s jowls shook uncontrollably as he bumbled through a speech on the speed of the economic recovery. I looked around me, ‘Yeah,’ I thought, ‘this abandoned shopping centre is a beacon for a fair future for all.’ I snorted under my breath at my own sarcasm before turning back to the screen.

Something was wrong.

The Prime Minister’s piggy eyed squint had been replaced by a wide eyed terror, he tried to continue with his speech but his mouth just opened and closed like a fish out of water. Foam began to cling to the corners of his lips as the fish-like movements were replaced by a clenched jaw as the electricity racing up his arms forced all of his muscles to contract. The podium began to smoke and hiss, loud enough for it to be heard through the television. I had seen this look of anguish before; when the electricity had been coursing through Mark's battered body shortly before he died. The terror and revulsion leapt to my throat from my stomach, the cocktail of painkillers I had been on since the ballroom hadn't helped. I heaved and spat onto the cracked tiles as Jeanette and Doc stood, transfixed by the convulsions and contortions of the dying man. As his aides ran to him, the all too familiar sound of machine gun fire rang out around the conference room.

I wiped my mouth with the back of my hand and turned back to the screen, as transfixed by the unfolding bloodbath as Doc and Jeanette. When the smoke cleared from the screen the podium and deceased Prime Minister had been cleared away, in their place, a tall, slender man in a black suit stood, his piercing blue eyes staring out from the screen and deep into my soul. "Ladies and gentlemen," he began, "I am Jacob Wyndham; you need not fear me or my organisation. The established political class had become corrupt and lazy. We are here to rid you of their burden. We are the Phoenix." It was impossible. I had seen this man Wyndham before. He had died in the hangar, Adrienne had killed him. I was there, I had felt his blood on my face.

I sank to my knees. None of what had just happened was possible, but in one fell swoop, the Phoenix now had control of the country, and the technology behind them to maintain it. Wyndham was speaking again, "Now, I said before that you had nothing to fear from us. That was true, there are, however, people who will see your safety compromised in order to return you to the yoke of greedy, lazy politicians."

My heart throbbed in my ears, head reeling from the vomiting and the craziness which was unfolding in front of my eyes. I knew who Wyndham meant when he spoke of people who would oppose the Phoenix.

Me.

Chapter Twenty-Three

Doc grabbed my arm and pulled me away from the screen, "Come on," he said, "we've got to move."

Joe's disembodied laughter followed us from the old screens which clung to the columns shedding their plaster.

I nodded, numb with confusion. I stumbled after him and Jeanette, who he was pulling by the hand through the darkness. I didn't know or really care where we were going, everything felt hopeless, with all the destitution created around us in this part of town; and undoubtedly repeated in cities everywhere, all Wyndham had to do was put a bounty on my head so huge the people couldn't resist and that would be it. Game over.

Doc and Jeanette had run down a corridor between two abandoned shops, having kicked the broken signs aside and picked their way through the shattered neon strip lights which covered the floor. They turned and beckoned me to follow, their figures bathed in the bright white light from an unseen room to the right about fifty metres away from me. I took one final look back towards the store where so many lives had been taken so swiftly mere moments ago, then jogged to catch up to my counterparts.

It took my eyes a couple of seconds to adjust from the darkness of the corridor to the brightness of the room. When they did, I saw we were standing in a wide room, tools lay haphazardly on the stainless steel bench which ran alongside the pristine antique blue and silver Ford Mustang which glimmered beneath the strip lights. It took my breath away, even in the midst of the chaos we were running from, I couldn't help but step back and nod appreciatively at the stunning specimen of car before me.

Doc was already at the driver's seat, with the passenger side door open and waiting to receive me. "Come on," he bellowed, "we don't have much time!" I took a look back to Jeanette, her face downcast and eyes red.

"What about you?" I asked, my eyes meeting hers.

Jeanette looked down to the shiny garage floor. "I'm not coming," she said, a slight tremor crept into her voice. "This building contains so many details on the Faceless, that if the Phoenix were to find it, so many more innocent lives could be lost."

I nodded, that made sense, there had been so much bloodshed in this insane war that the slaughter of any more innocents made the bile rise in my throat. "So, why do you have to stay behind?" I asked.

Jeanette nibbled her thumbnails, eyes fixed on her feet. "There's a secret room at the top of the centre, it contains a control panel that is wired to bombs in the concrete we installed as a last resort. There's no automated system. We didn't have the technology." A resigned bitterness had crept into her voice, the regret that it had all come down to this. "But," she said, stiffening with a sudden resolve, "I can at least buy you some time."

I shook my head in disbelief, hoping against hope that what I was hearing was nothing more than the latest twist in this ever unravelling nightmare. Jeanette looked up from her feet, her blue eyes swimming with tears. “Just promise me one thing Michael,” she stuttered drawing deep, shuddering breaths, “take those bastards down.”

“Isn’t there–” I began, trying desperately to fish for the words that could save another innocent person from an unnecessary death, but Jeanette shook her head, predicting the idea that was so unforthcoming in my mind.

“No, Michael, there isn’t,” she said, smiling through her tears, “I’ve just lost everything, everyone I’ve ever cared about has been taken away from me, and, ever since the Phoenix killed my husband all those years ago, I’ve been fighting for justice.” She paused. “Now I just can’t fight anymore. At least I’ll be back with my family soon.” A peaceful smile spread gradually over her face. “But I can still do one last thing, so go, now, and I’ll try to take as many as I can with me.” Jeanette removed a long barrelled pistol from her belt, clicking a magazine into place as she turned away from me to run back down the corridor.

Chapter Twenty-Four

I stayed motionless for a moment after she had departed, staring numbly at the space Jeanette's diminutive frame had vacated. The gunshots that echoed down the corridor jolted me violently back into the moment with a huge surge of adrenaline. Doc held down the horn of the Mustang again, "Come on, Michael, we have to move!" he yelled above the revving engine as the car began to squirm as the power from the engine began to battle with the handbrake. I sprinted the four steps from where I was to the passenger side and slammed the door behind me. Doc dropped the handbrake and the Mustang shot out of the garage, tortured tyres squealing as we blasted out into the murky urban dawn. A couple of shabbily dressed homeless people huddled round a brazier looked up briefly as our bolt of blue and silver lightning screeched past. The speedometer nudged ninety as flames spat from the exhaust as Doc wrenched the Mustang into top gear and we sped forward. "Glove box, now!" Doc yelled as bright lights illuminated the interior, bullets whistling through the air from behind. I fumbled the metallic silver button to the glove box as two bullets cracked into the rear window, shattering it and sending a shower of broken glass into the cabin. A trickle of warmth spread its way down the back of my neck, I knew without checking that I had a piece of glass jaggedly piercing the back of my ear. A matte silver tray slid out from the glove box with a compact sub-machine gun and magazine impressed into the foam tray. I wrenched it out of the holder, snapped the magazine into the butt of the gun and leant out of the window.

Two sleek black Mercedes sped up behind us, blackened windscreens reflecting the streetlights and the smears of blue and grey that had crept into the early morning sky. The passengers of the Mercedes leant out of their windows and fired towards us. I ducked, more bullets flying narrowly past my face. I squeezed the trigger of the machine gun, wind stinging my eyes as the trickle of blood increased its procession down my back and made my head spin. One of the spray of bullets managed to strike the front tyre of one of the chasing pack, causing it to flip and roll, flames licking at the underside as the rims scraped along the road; the driver fighting for control before the final rolls brought it to a halt on its roof. Another car, previously hidden by the first two careered into the side of the upturned chaser, causing the pair of them to explode into a fireball.

Doc whooped with exhilaration as he glanced back at the unfolding catastrophe behind us. His joy was short lived, however, as the explosion was dwarfed by one further behind. Jeanette must have made it to the trigger system because the shopping centre suddenly erupted volcanically, sending a huge shockwave down out from the city centre, sending chunks of concrete and shards of glass out high into the dawn sky. We sat back in our seats, slumped in a soup of emotion, overjoyed that at least half of our pursuers had been removed by the petrol rich flames which lapped at the road behind us, but stunned by the fact that Jeanette had to be engulfed by the ever expanding cloud of flame and rubble for us to escape.

The hail of bullets screamed through the air, bringing us out of our mutual misery, puncturing the back of the Mustang and causing sparks to leap into the early morning air. Doc wrestled with the steering wheel, sawing it back and forth, as the back of the car snaked out of control as the surface beneath the tyres became increasingly slippery. Doc swore viciously as he wrenched the wheel back and forth. The reason for the reduction in grip became apparent when I peered over the dashboard to see a shiny snaking oil slick which had been poured onto the road by two hooded men who threw their lighters into the ever expanding pool of oil just as we entered it. The flames erupted from the dark tarmac and lapped frantically at the underside of the Mustang. Doc stamped his foot to the floor, sending a squeal from the back tyres as they struggled for grip on the oily surface. The only thing the added power achieved was to send us into an uncontrolled slide along the flaming oil. The tyres burst in the heat, generating more sparks which ignited more of the oil we had carried with us. Ahead, a roadblock had been set up; two giant and ominous black Cadillac Escalades were parked with their noses together, tinted windows rolled up, with gunmen using the cars as cover. Doc hit the brakes and we began to skid slowly to a halt, the metal rims of the Mustang screaming as they locked up and skipped over the tarmac in a shower of more sparks.

Chapter Twenty-Five

Jeanette ran down the corridor firing blindly into the darkness. As she left Michael Wolf and Doc, she felt a pang of sorrow at the certainty she wouldn't survive the next few minutes. The rapid chatter of machine gun fire danced in the air around her as she slid on her knees, finding cover behind one of the concrete pillars. The upper concourse was alight with flashes of machine gun barrels, chipping away at the plaster surface of the pillar she was behind. Jeanette knew that she couldn't stay hidden forever. If not for her, to get the explosion set so Michael and Doc could escape.

She thought back to the day her son went missing, the clothes he was wearing as he went to work in the morning, the smile on his face. He had always loved Phoenix technology, so for him to get a job there was a dream come true for him. She felt the warm sensation of pride she had felt that morning, and the cold, sinking dread when he didn't come back. Jeanette had scoured internet forums, looking for other people who had lost loved ones in connection with the Phoenix. To her surprise she found hundreds of mothers, fathers, sons, daughters, husbands, wives and partners who had all lost loved ones. One such person, she only ever knew as Mark, recruited her to the Faceless, and together they delved into the secret world which the Phoenix had constructed out of the limelight of all the glamourous product launches and shiny advertisements. A world which was so much darker and dangerous than the watching world could ever have dreamt.

As soon as the news broke that Mark had been killed, Jeanette assumed leadership of the Faceless; knowing all the while that once she had joined the Faceless, the only way out was death. Even though she had taken a lot of time to familiarise herself with the knowledge of her impending death, in this moment, a huge stab on anguish writhed in her belly. She hated the Phoenix, she hated Mark, she wished she had never heard of the Faceless, but most of all, she wished she could have seen her son, Jonathan, one final time. Burning with a furious anger, she reloaded her gun and stepped out from behind her pillar, firing four times. The bullets flew up into the darkness of the upper concourse, thumping into two unseen assailants who promptly dropped their guns over the side of the upper platform, landed with a clatter on the floor, metres away from Jeanette. She lunged forward to the dropped guns firing upward at the remaining assailants, in a hope that it would be enough of a distraction for her to pick up one of the discarded weapons and get up towards the fire escape.

She made it to the fire escape, avoiding more of the gunfire that trailed her fleeting footsteps as she crashed into the stairwell. Two masked men in black suits were waiting at the top of the first flight of stairs. Jeanette dispatched them with ease before they had chance to aim their guns at her. She clambered up the steps to the next floor, where the men had been standing, grabbed a grenade off their belt, removed the pin and threw it through the door to the upper concourse, before hiding back in the corridor. There was a flurry of activity and swearing as the remaining gunmen on the upper concourse tried desperately to evade the grenade, but to no avail. The resulting fireball chased her along the next flight of stairs to the roof. Jeanette burst through the hatch to the roof before seeing ten men in the same black suits at various points on the roof, blocking Jeanette's access to the air vent in which the Faceless had hidden the detonator for the building.

Jeanette removed the magazine from her machine gun and fumbled for a new one. She swore under her breath behind the air vent at the other end of the roof. She was out of ammo, and a long way from the detonator. Jeanette swallowed the bitter nausea that rose in her throat and began to creep across the rough bitumen, small stones and broken glass cutting into her hands. She bit her lip as the pain began to bite, but continued to crawl behind the silent sentries of the roof. Halfway toward the vent which contained the detonator, Jeanette unthinkingly brushed an ancient glass bottle aside, causing it to spin and shatter on the concrete perimeter which ran around the top of the roof. The sentries all spun around, their machine guns snapped up to their shoulders, barrels pointing down to Jeanette's crouching figure. A sudden explosion from the street below caused the guns to waver, as the guards looked over their shoulders as the flames and smoke began to rise. Jeanette seized this opportunity, scrambling off her haunches, and ran toward the air vent containing the detonator. One of the guards called out as he spun round from the chaos below to see her running towards the vent.

Another clatter of gunfire followed Jeanette towards the vent; a searing pain in her side caught her as she dived towards the vent. She made it, with one hand covering an ever expanding patch of crimson that began to sap her strength as she fumbled with the keys to initiate the countdown sequence. She bitterly cursed the fact that the detonator had been positioned on the roof, with no chance of escape before the thirty second countdown was up. The gunmen tried to follow her into the vent, but couldn't as a protective sheet of thick, bulletproof steel slid out of the floor behind her.

The ticking began to echo around the tiny chamber which was to become her mausoleum, counting down the seconds to the inevitable conclusion. Jeanette's mind began to wander from her situation, the burning, stinging wound in her side taking over all her thoughts. The warmth of the blood which seeped from her side began to soothe her as she shuddered into a state of unconsciousness. As the dream state began to take effect, Jeanette could have sworn a face appeared close to hers. David. She reached her hand out to caress the face which lingered in front of hers, their eyes meeting, a sad smile played across his lips.

"David," she whispered, the dryness of her mouth making her voice rasping and harsh, "I've missed you so much." The metallic tang of the blood rose in her throat, bubbling at the corners of her mouth as the bullet wound in her side sapped the last of her strength. "I love–" but she never finished her sentence, as the building beneath her began to disintegrate as the roar of explosives laced into the foundations began to take effect; burying Jeanette in a cloud of fire, concrete and steel.

Chapter Twenty-Six

The rough grab on my forearm awoke me with a start. I was upside down in the smoking wreckage of the Mustang, which was on its roof. I hoped it was Doc who was pulling me to safety from the car, but as I looked to my left Doc's unconscious body was being hauled away by a masked man in black armour. I closed my eyes again and allowed these masked men to carry us out of the car, I didn't have the energy to fight back, the bleeding from behind my ear had left me drowsy and nauseous, at the very least these people had got us out of the car. Limply I was loaded onto the shoulders of the guard before being dumped in the back of one of the Cadillacs. Doc was dropped lifelessly into the boot next to me, dirty smudges of blood and oil covered his face. Both his eyes were almost swollen shut where he had hit the steering wheel as we had collided with the other Escalade; which was being moved into position near the Mustang in order to fake a crash. "Right, that'll do lads, let's torch this place and get out of here!" called one of the gruff voices from outside. The doors of our Escalade slammed shut and the engine rumbled into life. As we pulled away from the scene I craned my neck to see the crash site explode into a brilliant orange ball of flame, covering the tracks of us and the Phoenix guards that had been there.

I rested my head back on the plush carpets of the Escalade, a tight knot of fear twisting in my guts, resigned to the situation and relieved but slightly disturbed they hadn't killed us on sight. Whatever Joe and Wyndham had planned for us, I had the distinct feeling that a quick death would be a walk in the park. I looked Doc up and down, he hadn't moved since the guards dumped him next to me. I gave him a sharp shove in the shoulder. "Come on Doc, wake up!" I hissed, shaking him more violently as he groggily began to groan. His eyes struggled against their puffy prisons, opening to a squint. "Shh," I whispered as he began to stir, "we're in the back of a car, no idea where we're going, but I think it's going to take us closer to Adrienne." He nodded slowly, and lowered his head to the carpet. I watched him settle briefly and then followed suit.

The miles dragged on, each second twisting the knot of fear tighter in my guts as we moved closer to whatever dark destiny awaited us at the end of the journey. My mind drifted back to Mark, standing in my living room, what felt like an entirely different lifetime ago; his notebook, his ramblings, how I derided him without a second's thought. The twisting knot in my stomach was joined by another sensation; the guilt of his death on my hands cut me like a knife. I sank further into the boot of the Escalade and gave in to the silent sobs that pulled my chest and stung my eyes. The hopelessness of the situation rendered me immobile, paralysed and unable to avoid the fate I believed was coming for me.

"You know," Doc began croakily, "the reason you called the organisation you set up 'the Phoenix'?" He squinted through his purple hooded eyes.

I tried to shush him through my sobs, but he continued, "You called it the Phoenix because the inventions you were building were to pull humanity out of the mess it had created for itself. Wars and natural disasters had just about torn civilisation apart; you believed that," he took a deep shuddering breath, "you believed that even in the darkest days, something better could grow from the ashes."

My sobs subsided as I listened, Doc's croaky story had soothed my guilt. I nodded, feeling the back of my head as the movement had sent a shot of pain down my neck. Doc reached out to put his hand on my shoulder. "Never forget that," he stared imploringly into my face, "never. The Phoenix stood for hope, ambition, and the drive to be something better than the worst circumstances you find yourself in." His smile shone through his broken face. "Ok then," he rolled onto his back, "rest up, we've got a long day ahead."

With that he shuffled into a more comfortable position in the boot and drifted off, snoring through his broken nose.

Chapter Twenty-Seven

The car rolled to a gradual halt as I had just begun to drift off into a light, wary sleep. The gravel crunched as the hefty Escalade rolled off the road into the yard. Even though I couldn't see, I knew instinctively I had been here before. The fear snaked into the pit of my stomach, squirming through my guts and making me shake uncontrollably. My legs were grabbed forcefully as I was pulled roughly from the boot. I stood shaking, the burn from the car's carpet stinging the cuts on my face. They removed Doc from the car with the same amount of care and finesse they had shown me. I stole a quick glance across at him, he didn't look any better in the daylight, his broken nose was squashed to the left and cuts and bruises were beginning to scab over. At least his eyes were a little less swollen. I sighed with relief, before a bag was roughly shoved over my head and my hands were tied behind my back.

We were marched roughly along a corridor, our stumbling feet and the rhythmic stomp of the guards' boots rattling along the grated metal floors; although we were blindfolded, I could tell we weren't far from the main atrium of the Phoenix science and development facility where Joe had murdered my wife. The memory of my last time in this building rocked me and my legs went from under me as my breathing became short and panicked. The guard who had been marshalling me down the cramped hallways grabbed my collar and dragged me along the grated metal and into a cell.

The bag hadn't been removed from my head, the rough fibres began to catch on the cuts to my face, as I moved to try and free myself from their entangling embrace, they pulled at the wounds, stinging and burning until more blood began to ooze from them. I began to wriggle my hands free; the bonds which held them hadn't been secured too tightly, so fifteen minutes later, and with a bit of persuasion, my hands were free. Gingerly I removed the bag from my head, wiped the blood and dirt from my cheeks and looked around. This cell was slightly bigger than the last one, with a mirrored finish to both the side walls. I paced up and down the centre of the cell. In my mind I could see the observers hidden behind the mirrored walls, clipboards at the ready, noting my responses and reactions to everything that was going to happen to me.

Within moments of my hands and face being freed, one of the mirrored glass screens began to show a film of another cell, quite possibly the one adjacent to mine, where Adrienne's battered and bloodied body hung limply from the ceiling, arms outstretched, clamped back to the walls with heavy metal manacles. My breaths became shorter; an angry red flush began to creep up my neck as I stared at the grotesque, beaten body before me. My elevated heartbeat roared in my ears as a numb anger began to sweep over me, the shrieks and yells that emanated from my body felt estranged from my vocal chords, as if they didn't belong to me. I pounded on the glass, over and over again until the impact from the toughened glass reverberating through my fists shook me to my bones.

Joe's silky smooth sneer crept into the cell, his voice like barbed honey making my blood boil. "You know," he began, "human beings have brought the planet to its knees, in a stupid, bloody and brutal race, but do you know the one resource no-one's thought to exploit yet?" He chuckled to himself over the speakers hidden in my cell; it was almost as if he was surrounding me, suffocating me in a fog of confusion which accompanied his words. I couldn't get Adrienne's face out of my mind.

"Well… go on, guess!" Joe's impatient tone stirred me into concentrating on his question. My mind raced; as far as I had been concerned, recently humanity had pillaged most of the planet in its relentless search for supremacy, oil reserves were dwindling to nothing, mines were running out of coal and gas, and the rainforests had been destroyed to make room for new cities. I shook my head, clueless.

"I have no idea." I muttered with my head bowed.

Joe's insane chuckle began to rise in his throat. I could hear him try to stifle it unsuccessfully. "It's the mind!" he exclaimed, "the human mind, a resource which has remained untapped since the dawn of time, broadly because the people in possession of these minds were very reluctant to allow other people to tap their minds to see what they can find. Now, however, we live in a world where people are so content to share their thoughts on virtually anything on social media, and in new ways thanks to the technology we provide them, they're remarkably less bothered by bigger issues."

My heart began to slide inexorably towards my feet, the slow, sinking feeling dropping into the pit of my stomach. The pieces of the puzzle I hadn't quite been able to put together slowly began to fall into place.

It all made sense; this had always been the plan, the chip in my hand had been making me forget the warpath Joe and I had been on, they had used me, controlled me, kept me docile until the time was right to show my return to the world. I guessed that moment couldn't be far off, now that Joe was explaining his plan to me. The Phoenix would need a scapegoat, a figurehead to blame if everything went wrong for them; and after all, who better than the man behind the ideas in the first place?

The tears began to roll down my cheeks, hot and stinging as they mingled with the dirt on my face.

"What happens to the people who resist you?" I stammered, afraid I already knew the answer.

Joe's chuckle snaked from the speakers secreted away in the cell. I hated that chuckle; it had become a sure sign that my worst fears were about to be realised. "Not many people have been privy to this level of the organisation, but those who do we replace, with more," he paused, "compliant versions of themselves. Soon that won't be how we deal with them though. The plan is proceeding on schedule."

I shuddered, remembering back to the office in the hangar. How mk. 2 and the blue eyed man, Wyndham, had been there. How Wyndham had gone on to somehow kill the Prime Minister and take his place, live on TV, despite Adrienne slitting his throat.

I frowned, the semi-healed cuts on my face burned as my forehead contracted. "Replace them how?" I asked, knowing the answer again, it just sounded so insane in my head that I almost needed Joe's confirmation to make it real.

“Clones,” the cool, matter of fact reply came back over the secreted speakers, “we have the technology, and the ability to upload your personality to a new body thanks to the data collected by the ComChip. You met your replacement; he was almost ready to take your place, before Adrienne killed him.” The embittered sigh into the microphone was audible, even if Joe had tried to hide it.

I stifled a laugh, even in the face of everything, the idea that the Phoenix had been so blindingly short sighted they’d only made a single clone of me forced a slight burst of laughter. Joe heard my snort of derision. “What?” he snapped.

“Nothing, nothing,” I muttered, cradling my chest against the raging pain inside, “you only made one clone of me? Frankly I’m insulted, Joseph!”

Joe’s silence seemed to hang heavy in the air as I waited anxiously for him to reply. Without another word the wall opposite me lit up. Two photographs slid into view. My heart began to thump against my ribs’ vice-like grip. I was staring back at my own face, projected against the wall. Alongside it, the man called Wyndham’s face appeared.

“Now, why would you think there’s only one of you?” Joe’s conceited tone only served to pump more adrenaline into my system.

As I watched, stunned, the photo of Wyndham began to change. The cold, calculating blue eyes faded to a dark chestnut brown. My eyes. The hair began to thin and grow out, matching mine. The teeth became a greyer shade of white.

“So what?” I mocked, hoping to mask the fear I knew what was coming next, “you’ve just learnt how to use Photoshop and want to show it off? You’ve swapped a few of his facial features and made him look like me, what's that got to do with anything?"

Joe's chuckle crackled through the speakers again. "Just watch, Michael, just watch." The false soothing tone made me shake uncontrollably.

My picture began to change, morph into Wyndham's until the pictures had changed places. My greying, thin hair began to thicken and shorten. My teeth became whiter and my eyes changed from brown to blue. The horrible, sinking realisation of what was happening began to sink in.

Beneath the swapped photos, a small panel had appeared, glowing green. The words "DNA MATCH" flickered on and off within them.

"Do you see now? Do you understand?" Joe's voice quivered with manic excitement. "We haven't got ONE of you, we have hundreds! We give them contact lenses for their eyes, a ComChip for their thoughts and send them out into the world. It's what we did with you."

The last words of his sentence hung heavy like a cloud over my head, pushing it down into my hands. "What?" I murmured, my disbelief of what I was hearing shone through. I couldn't even disguise it anymore.

"You did die in that explosion Michael," Joe began, "well, technically. Your body survived, but you were declared brain dead. We cryogenically froze you so we had a fresh supply of DNA for our new versions of you. You see, we didn't make ONE copy, you ARE a copy, with hundreds of brothers around the world. We put them in positions of power, where we could influence them through the ComChip and they could then consequently influence the people they work with. Governments, businesses, whole nations under our control! They may not be directly in the public gaze but in the ears of the people who are. When things go wrong, the people directly in the public eye get the blame, they get replaced and your clones get closer to the new people."

"And the whole horrible cycle starts again." I groaned. The tears stung my eyes. Michael's eyes. "So what was different with Wyndham?" I asked. "Why did you not replace the Prime Minister with another Prime Minister and let Wyndham get close to him again?"

Joe paused, it may have been only a couple of seconds, but it felt like an eternity. Finally he spoke, "Wyndham was necessary, the Prime Minister had people investigating us and we had to ensure that we could shut down his enquiry before it started. We orchestrated a few disappearances before Wyndham became PM, people who had been on the committees and panels which were investigating us. Then as Wyndham stepped into the role, they miraculously returned to his cabinet, just without the inclination to investigate us anymore."

"Convenient," I spat.

"Incredibly," Joe laughed. "Come along, I have something to show you."

Chapter Twenty-Eight

Along the bank of screens, two on the far end caught my eye. My heart began to rise from my feet as I could just about make out the figures of Adrienne and Doc in their separate cells. Doc was pacing forcefully up and down as I had, whilst Adrienne sat cross-legged on the bench along the wall of her cell.

A rough grab on either upper arm pulled me to my feet. My legs shook, even under my slighter frame. The probable weeks of imprisonment and lack of space to stretch my legs had left my body weak. I stood there, in my dirty clothes, scratched and bruised under the watchful eyes of white coated technicians who stood on a balcony running around the edge of the room. Beneath them more drones typed furiously while the blue light from the screens rained down into their unblinking eyes.

Joe's voice came from high above my head, I looked up to see him push aside two technicians and lean over the balcony. "Only one?" he cackled. "Michael my dear friend, if you think we were so short sighted as to only reproduce you once, you are sorely mistaken!"

"You know what I mean, Michael," Joe snapped, but he took a deep breath, stared at me with his piercing green eyes and began. "As soon as you decided that the direction I was taking the science and technologies department was the wrong way, I found backing somewhere else. Some other people with more money and fewer...," he hesitated over the words, rolling it around his lips before spitting it out, "moral qualms." His stare didn't waver, even for a moment. "We set up another facility, far away from here, and began syphoning off funds and technical schematics to some of your latest work to begin weaponising them. Soon enough our projects began to attract buyers, and parts of our technology have been used to fight, and win, wars all over the world."

Parts of what Joe was saying made sense. He had stolen from me, lied to me and tried to kill me, all in the pursuit of whatever he saw as his warped Utopia. This however, didn't explain why he had begun cloning, why he was now targeting the public with technology designed to enslave them. I said as much, as I stared up at him.

"It's simple really," came the reply, "our clients decided that instead of creating wars and controlling both sides, it would be easier to sell seemingly harmless technology to people, control them, lull them into a state of apathetic addiction to us and slowly remove their human autonomy."

I sank to my knees. The impossibility of turning the tide against the terrible faceless puppeteers became all too real. "What about the people who oppose you?" I spat.

Joe smiled, a little chuckle escaped him again. "We replace them. That's where the clones come in, were you not paying attention Michael? Right now, there are versions of Mark and Jeanette and countless others ready to walk back into the homes and lives of their families, all over the world, subservient, peaceful and no longer burdened by the things they can't change. Think about it," a devilish light danced in his emerald eyes, "a world without dissent, without opposition, without conflict or strife!"

I had figured as much, it had obviously been the plan with me before Adrienne intervened. In that moment I realised how much she had risked to save me and my heart sank further towards my feet. As I thought about her, I thought back to how much of her childhood I had missed and how Joe had become the cuckoo in my nest and twisted her into a killer. She had changed though, she saved my life, fought against everything that Joe and his shady investors had instilled in her. The swell of pride forced me back to my feet, my legs no longer shaking as I stared into Joe's cold green eyes.

The realisation of the whole sickening plan and how much it had taken a grip on people flooded in. All around the world people had begun to retract into a comforting bubble, provided by the technologies of the Phoenix. All the while Joe and his investors sat in the shadows, watching, waiting. Pulling the marionette strings. When the time was right they began to siphon the individuality from them, moulding them into the dispensable drones that were ready to be used. Anaesthetised by the changing process, they were unable to fight back; and when people like Mark or Jeanette discovered the truth they were silenced, replaced and the process continued as normal.

"No," I spat, my confidence beginning to return as I spoke "No. You've got it all wrong. Everything. You're removing the beating heart of humanity, tearing its soul out and burning it so you can control the ashes." It seemed so futile when I said it out loud. Everything the Phoenix was doing just to dominate, their cloying overconfidence that no-one had the power to speak up and fight. I thought about Adrienne and Doc, Mark and Jeanette, and the countless nameless people who had tried before. They hadn't had leadership, direction, in some cases knowledge the others even existed. This was going to change. All I had to do to start the change was free Adrienne and Doc.

A silence fell over the room as I finished speaking. The hush was deafening, all eyes were trained on me, scanning me for weakness. They wouldn't find any. My resolve had been strengthened by the adrenaline flowing through my veins. Joe stomped along the balcony, his shoes rattling off the metal flooring and echoing up to the cavernous ceiling. As he was marching along above me, I stole a glance at the room I was in. It was larger than my cell, with space for observers to mill around comfortably as some were while I watched. The door was a reachable distance from me, heavy, opaque and metal.

Joe was at ground level before I could formulate a plan of escape.

"Soul and humanity?" He pressed his face right up to mine, breath hot and angry on my skin. He laughed. "Wake up Michael! They don't exist anymore, money and power have taken over, it's cutthroat but it works." He smiled sadistically. "I'm planning on killing you tonight, here in this building, so give it your best shot." He curled his lip upward into a sneer. "With all your soul and humanity." He spat the words back at me, as if they physically disgusted him, the taste of them bitter on his tongue. "The fact of the matter is this; we are the hand that rocks the cradle, the comforter in an increasingly scary world. Everything you were, are, will be and have is all down to our design." He backed away from me, arms outstretched. He wheeled around the room, psyching himself up in front of the crowd of technicians.

I tried to keep my face still, even though I could feel the frown begin to crawl across it. Why would he tell me he was going to kill me and not just do it? The sinking sensation had returned to my stomach, there was more to Joe's game, more he needed me for. I wasn't expendable quite yet.

Joe gestured toward the two neighbouring screens, Adrienne and Doc sat silently in their separate cells. Doc had stopped pacing and was sitting staring blankly at the wall opposite. "You see them?" he said, waggling a finger in their direction, "they're both waiting on you. They think," he chuckled again, "they both think, that you're going to save them!"

"I am." The indignant determination bolstered my voice.

"You're going to try," Joe's playful reply filled me with a cold dread. "Both cells are filling with a poison gas, they can't smell it or taste it and in a few minutes they'll fall asleep and never wake up. Their only chance is you."

Joe had wheeled away from me, dawdling along with his hands behind his back.

"Why?" The embittered question was out of my mouth before I could stop it.

Joe's pacing paused, he turned on his heels and strolled back towards me. He shrugged, "because I can. You're just an experiment." He smiled, jabbing his finger into my chest, "We want to see how much a human can withstand before we find a breaking point and gives in to us. We've taken a lot from you, your wife, your name, your identity, and now either your confidant or your daughter." My heartbeat thundered in my ears making my head swim nauseatingly. Everything had been systematically dismantled just so that my tolerances could be examined. Our lives meant nothing to them. We were merely lab rats in a maze. One wrong move and they would snuff our lives out as easily as switching off a light. A churlish grin spread across his face as he wheeled away.

Joe carried on speaking, but I wasn't listening, the cold sweat poured from my forehead as the sickening lump choked me. Anger had swept away my earlier confidence, replacing it with the cold dread that Joe's words had inspired. One of the technicians rose from the bank of screens and headed wordlessly for the door. Joe continued to ramble on, his back to me as he carried on walking away. Before he could react, I snatched at the metal chair and swung it at his head with all the force I could muster. It caught him with a crack, sending him crumpled to the floor. The technicians dropped what they had been carrying and swarmed towards me. A few more wild swings of the chair bought me the space from the reach of the technicians who flocked toward me and time to make a break for the door.

Chapter Twenty-Nine

The corridor behind the door I fell through was bright and airy, with white walls which stretched out in front of me. I scrambled to my feet and began running, the clatter of gunfire chased me, the faint whizz of bullets fizzed narrowly past my ears. There hadn't been any guards in the room with Joe. I guessed they had been standing outside when I'd surprised them by flying past. I wasn't going to stop and check, the gunfire made certain of that. My head was on fire trying make some semblance of sense as to what Joe had revealed to me. Adrienne and Doc's faces danced nauseatingly behind my eyes, their sad, broken faces staring unsighted back at me. "I'm sorry," I muttered under my breath, "I'm sorry." The bitter, angry tears stung my face.

A sudden, dull throbbing began to hum above me, stopping me in my tracks. It grew to a crescendo as I stared upward. The metal underbelly of a helicopter glided into view. The glass roof above me shattered as three figures in black crashed through it. The gloved hand was firm but friendly on my shoulder, I looked up to see a pair of green eyes peering down at me from behind a Perspex visor. He reached his hand up to his mask and slid it down past his mouth.

"Adrienne!" I spluttered urgently.

"Miss A?" He yelled over the chatter of the still hovering helicopter. "We've been tracking her since her emergency beacon was set off! We'll get her, Doc is on the third floor; if you hurry, you'll easily get to him."

I nodded, shaken. The chatter of gunfire had been silenced by the man's colleagues who had made short work of the two guards who had been shooting at me.

The push from the gloved hand set me running again. My heavy legs thumped along the polished black floor as I pushed past the burning in my chest. I rounded the corner and lurched into the stairwell, my breathing heavy, head spinning from the lack of oxygen. Joe's voice echoed through the speakers.

"People always want security and safety. That's all that we're doing," he cajoled, "providing their bubble, leading them away from the things that could harm them."

"Save me the sales pitch!" I croaked. My dry mouth and heaving chest made every word feel like a battle, but I pushed on, "You can say all the shit you want, try and spin it to the public in any way you want, but it doesn't change the fact you and your overlords are murderous bastards who see the people you 'protect' as cattle to be farmed to line your own pockets."

Joe laughed, his disembodied chortling echoed off the bare concrete walls and floors. "Who are the people going to believe, Michael? You? We're everywhere, we are every*one*! They'll write you off, the way they wrote off Mark, and Jeanette and all the other individuals who got too close to the truth. After tomorrow, you'll be just another lunatic rambling in the face of progress. There will be no-one to challenge us, no-one to stop us, we will have our victory!"

Tomorrow – what was happening tomorrow? Why would no-one be able to stop them after? All the questions crashed around in my head again. I was spinning, my ears were ringing, lack of oxygen biting harder now. I lumbered up the stairs to the third level, Joe's taunts still ringing in my ears; his laughter a constant shadow chasing me upwards.

I burst into the third floor hallway. The door cannoned back off the wall and into my shoulder. The pain stunned me temporarily but I carried on, knowing I was closer to the room where Doc was being held. The lights were flickering on this floor, everywhere else I had been in the building the lights had been belligerently blinding, here the strip lights flickered. The corridor was windowless, dark and wide enough for me not to be able to touch the walls. The low buzz from the faulty wires hummed around me. I pushed on into the gloom, slower now, more cautiously, saving my breaths.

The muffled screams drifted down the corridor to me. I couldn't tell if it was Doc or not, but the banging on the door and more hurried shouts told me they were running out of time.

Chapter Thirty

The urgency of the banging on the door pushed me forward. I broke back into a run, I followed the sound to the end of the corridor. A thick, wooden door stood between me and the source of the muffled shouts. I was so close I could tell that the man making the sounds was bound and gagged, using his shoulder to barge fruitlessly against the unrelenting wood.

"Doc?" I slapped my palm against the door, feeling the rough wood beneath my fingers. "Doc!"

The barging stopped. Doc's muffled shouts came as reply.

"It's OK Doc, it's alright, I'll get you out of here!" I said, relieved he was still alive, still fighting.

I scanned around for something to break the door down with. The gloom didn't help, and the flickering of the lights gave my eyes no time to adjust to what was around me. I snatched glances at the corridor when the lights came on and felt around in the darkness trying desperately to find something I could use to free Doc. Halfway down the hallway behind me, a glass case containing a fire axe and hose had been set into the wall. I ran to it, and punched the glass with all the strength I could manage. It shattered around my feet, stinging my fist. I felt the warm tingle of blood begin to stream from my hand. I reached for the axe, the blood made my grip slippery as I fumbled with the smooth plastic. I pulled it from the wall and sprinted back to the door.

"Get away from the door Doc!" I yelled, "I'm going to break in!"

No sound from within came as a reply.

The axe slid through my bloodied fingers as I swung it at the door. The strikes shook my arm and clattered against the unrelenting obstacle. The wood came away surprisingly easily, too easily. I stepped back, hands slippery and stinging from the shards of glass I hadn't removed. I stared through the intermittent light at what was blocking my path. The axe had taken chunks of wood away leaving the planks jagged and splintered. Beneath them a thick glass panel stood, resolute and undamaged.

The lights which had been flickering up to now hummed and sputtered into life, illuminating my dingy surroundings. Joe's voice floated down the hall, disembodied, from hidden speakers somewhere behind me.

"Well, you got to him, shame really. You were just out of time."

Doc was slumped against the glass, his head on his chest. His hands were bound together in his lap, wrists bloodied from where he had wrestled hurriedly against his bonds. The half of his face I could see had become purple and blotchy from sustained beatings, eye almost swollen shut. A string of scarlet saliva hung limply from his chin, leaking steadily from his nostrils and over the rag serving as a gag.

I sank to my knees and pressed my head against the cool pane of his tomb. I beat my hands against it, the dull thud of my weakened fists leaving little other than a bloody, smudged handprint. The strangled, bitter howl burst from me, agony tearing into my chest.

"He didn't have to die," I whispered, holding back the burning acid rising in my throat, "you didn't have to kill him."

Joe's reply came, short, stunted, uncaring, "No."

"Then, why?" I was numb, shaken from the loss of blood and uncontrollable anger swelling in my chest.

He chuckled to himself, "I told you before Michael, to see what happens when you push a human being past their point of no return. How they respond to their anger and grief is a tool we can use to control them and ensure we can restrain them."

Restrain them. The Phoenix's plan was simple, elegant and terrifying. Breed a world of compliance and kill anyone who dared to speak out.

"The Utopia you want – the dream world you're building, it won't happen," I spat. Adrenaline pushed me back to my feet, "I told you before, face to face, I will stop you. You didn't realise that when you take everything away from a person, they have nothing left to lose. I will be the last face you see. I will haunt your nightmares. DO YOU HEAR ME?" I roared, "I will fight you for these people!"

Joe sighed heavily his breath crackling on the speakers, "Michael, do you not see? Before the explosion, before I took over, we were curing a problem, constantly trying to improve on the faulty blueprint that is humanity. Just making cures and educating people in the hope that one day something would be better is a Utopian dream that never would happen. The people you want to fight us for? They're so contented in their numb state, they're happier for it. You've got to see that what we've built here is…" he savoured the word, "perfection."

"I don't see perfection," I said, my voice was harsh, barely above a whisper. "What you've created is subservience, you take away what makes people perfect and turn them into mindless consumers of whatever you see fit to shovel into them." I pointed at Doc's body. "If I don't want to be numb to this, I want to feel the anger, the sadness, the disappointment, because I know they're not the only things I can feel. I don't want to forget Doc; Jason," I corrected myself, "I remember his love for my daughter, his belief that there was something worth fighting for in people, and I will carry that with me for as long as I live. And another thing." I paused, staring defiantly up at a camera in the corner of the corridor, "I reserve the right to be a fuck up, to be imperfect, the same as any person should. We are not perfect by design; if we were, what would we live for?"

Joe was silent. I was left standing alone in the corridor. The lights returned to flickering with a low electric crackle. I bowed my head for a moment, took a final look back over my shoulder at where Doc was laying, and ran.

Chapter Thirty-One

I was in an unfamiliar corridor, another bright and clean one, obviously more used than the one Doc had just died in. The light burned against my eyes, the tears began to sting. I rounded a corridor and clattered into the three armed invaders from the helicopter. My heart began to pound in my chest, I shoved past them and stared at Adrienne, the Alpha squad had freed her. She was shaken, dishevelled and about as badly beaten as Doc had been, but she was alive. We stared at one other tentatively for a moment.

"Dad?" her voice was as shaky as she looked. "Jason?" She stared at me, hard, willing the right words to come back to her.

My chin hit my chest; I shook my head, unable to return her gaze.

Adrienne nodded slowly and sighed. Her breaths quivered with the grief she was trying to hold back. She stepped closer, we embraced, her cheek was wet against my neck.

"It's not your fault, Dad, it's not," she whispered between sobs. "We have to get out of here."

I nodded as we broke apart, one of the guards handed us spare machine guns they had brought with them. "The evacuation point is on the roof, we have a lot of floors between us and there, we have to move. Now."

The guards formed a perimeter around me, Adrienne fell in behind. We edged forward as a group, our pace on the verge of breaking into a run. We rounded a corner and were confronted by two guards who heard our footsteps. Our leader cut them down without giving them time to raise their guns. Their bodies hit the ground, pools of blood spreading from the wounds in their chests. We made it to a stairwell and began to make our climb. My legs were beginning to weaken by the time we reached the rooftop. The climb had been punishing and the repeated corkscrew motion on the stairs had made my legs wobble and my head spin.

We were high above the city, I stared around and it struck me that it was London. The wind whistled and whipped between the skyscrapers. The cold metallic edifices stretching like fingers upwards to graze the sky as the Thames snaked between them. We stared up in unison, breathing in the cold air and waiting for the hum of the helicopter's rotors. More guards lumbered through the door after us, guns raised, the chatter of gunfire rang out, high above the city's streets. A bullet whistled past me and struck one of the soldiers with us in the shoulder. He dropped onto his back clutching at the wound. Another took a bullet to the knee and collapsed as he tried to regain his balance. The final guard put up more of a fight. He took out two of our pursuers before a spray of bullets to the chest forced him back to the ledge. Another two shots to the chest made him stagger, trip and disappear over the railings.

The Phoenix's guard, dressed in black, swarmed onto the rooftop, finishing the two wounded guards. Twenty-five or more encircled Adrienne and me, weapons all pointing towards us. Joe stumped out of the doorway, past two of the Phoenix's men and into the circle with us. He stared hard at me.

"Good effort," he muttered, patting me on the shoulder, "Almo–"

He didn't finish his sentence. Adrienne had stepped between us and hit him, hard, with the butt of her gun. Joe's nose gave a huge crack and blood spurted down to cover his top lip, which had also been split by the blow. He staggered back, spat blood, clutching his nose. All the guns went up around us.

"No!" Joe spat the command through mouthfuls of blood. "Leave us."

The guards exchanged confused looks but dutifully disbanded their circle and marched back inside.

"There's no need for guns now," he said, raising his hands, "put them down."

Adrienne and I glanced at each other, neither of us willing to obey.

Joe shrugged. "Ok, I guess that wasn't ever going to happen."

I shook my head silently, staring down at his hunched figure as he tried to staunch the bleeding from his badly broken nose.

"What's happening tomorrow?" The question was out of me before I could stop it. "Why will no-one dare try and stop you after it?"

Joe laughed. A bubble of blood grew and burst as he snorted. "Utopia." He shouted above the gusting wind. A manic look had spread across his face, eyes wide with an insane delight. He smiled, stretching the split in his top lip even wider. A cascade of blood ran onto his teeth, leaving a yellowish stain smeared where he licked at it, "Tomorrow, Wyndham's government, and others around the world will announce that we will be providing everyone with an updated and much smaller version of the ComChip. It's been designed to look and feel less intrusive than the one on the hand, when in actual fact it will be wired into the nervous system at the base of the skull. When the switch on happens, we will have access to everyone and everything. We will be omnipotent and infinite. Anyone who refuses or begins to step outside their prescribed confines will be eliminated."

I nodded. The enormity of the task ahead of us lay before me. There was no way to stop the plan, no way to overturn the work that had already begun. The people would accept the upgrade because whoever was pulling their strings would suggest it to their subconscious, fuelling an unspoken desire to upgrade.

My panicked thoughts were interrupted by the rattling chatter from the helicopter. It loomed over us, forcing dust upwards from the rooftop. Spluttering and trying to keep the grit out of our eyes Adrienne and I staggered towards the rope ladder which had been lowered and was now swinging in the downdraft. The grit had been blown into the wounds from the emergency glass, making them burn and sting as the dust mingled with the tacky, almost dried blood.

I put it out of my mind and began to climb, the downdraft, the dust and the buffeting of the ladder conspired to make the ascent difficult. Adrienne had nimbly and gracefully swept up before me and was now leaning out of the helicopter trying to shout encouragement to me over the whirring rotors. A frown began to spread across her face, contorted into a shout. She pointed hurriedly over my shoulder, just as I felt a violent grab pulling at my leg. There was no way I could support the weight of myself and the assailant. The plastic rungs of the ladder slipped through my grasp and we were sent plummeting back to the roof. I landed with a thud on top of whoever had pulled me from the helicopter. I looked around, winded, knowing who I'd see. Joe staggered to his feet, clutching his ribs, breathing heavily.

"You didn't think it'd be that easy did you?" Joe cawed. More blood trickled from his nose and mouth. He brushed it away, retrieved his phone from his pocket and began to dial.

I leapt forward, tackling him back to the ground and knocking the phone out of his grasp. It skidded across the concrete. He tried to wriggle free but I pulled him back down and scrambled over him, putting myself between him and his phone. He charged, eyes wild, swinging his fists. He caught me with two frustrated punches to the head; I rocked backwards and tried to stay on my feet. My head was swimming. The helicopter whirred like a giant flying insect above us. He tried to hit me again but I was ready, I ducked and launched a hail of punches which crashed into Joe's jaw and chest. The blows made him stumble. My hands rang with pain from the impacts and the cuts which had begun to bleed again.

"No!" he screamed, "you will not beat me, you can't beat me!" He charged again, pushing me up against the railings. I peered over the side. Spots of Joe's blood spattered my cheek as he pushed me closer to the edge. His breath was hot and angry as he snarled at me. The pavement and the people beneath were tiny from here, I felt as though I was seeing them the way the power crazed maniac leering over me saw them. He was going to throw me to them, sending me down to re-join the ants from the heights of Olympus. Strength welled up within me. I pushed Joe off me and threw him over the edge. His hands made a clang as he scrambled to cling to the railings. Joe's arms shook as he dangled tantalisingly above the street. The wind and the downdraft from the helicopter battered us both. I stood on the ledge above him, panting hard. My head swam thanks to the beating I had taken. My hands were on my knees. I stared at Joe, my once best friend, clinging with all his might to the edge.

For the first time I saw the fear eclipse the maniacal high which had taken him over. He looked so small, so mortal. I reached over the edge. "Take my hand," I yelled above the helicopter.

He smiled; blood clung to the bottom half of his face, congealing in messy clumps around his lips and nostrils. "No. You're going to remember my face in your nightmares."

With that he let go. His laughter narrowly made it above the clatter of the rotors of the helicopter as he began his plummet down toward the street.

Chapter Thirty-Two

I stood there, motionless, hanging over the side of the building with my arm outstretched. The wind whirled around me. Everything seemed to move slowly as I watched Joe's laughing, soon to be corpse make its impact with the cold, hard pavement below. For a second everything felt incredibly still. Before I really knew what was going on, I was being pulled firmly but tenderly away from the rails, "Come on Dad, we need to get out of here!" Adrienne's voice was strangely calm, her breath warm against the cold wind on my neck.

I nodded, everything felt numb. Adrienne pulled me up into the back of the helicopter and it whirled away above the chaos unfolding on the street below. A small crowd had begun to form around Joe's body. The ambulance sirens blared out, screeching over the background hum of the city, their blue-lighted arrival all too late. Adrienne and I sat silently in the helicopter; she stared out of the window, nonchalantly watching the sun set, lengthening the shadows behind the palace of Westminster. Tomorrow the puppet government the Phoenix had installed would begin the implementation of the process Joe had developed. I watched Adrienne silently mourning Doc, her eyes red, cheeks wet with tears. She didn't bother trying to staunch their flow.

I crawled over to her, and pulled her into my arms and stroked her hair. Her silent sobs shook through my body as I cradled her close to me. “It’s ok,” I said, “we need to keep fighting, so that Jason, Mark, Jeanette and all the others didn’t die in vain.”

Adrienne twisted back to look me in the eye. A steely determination stiffened her resolve, “I want to kill them, all of them.” Her bitter tears rolled silently down her cheeks, she let them hang on her hardened jawline, grinding her teeth.

“No,” I said quietly, consoling her, “you’re angry, you’re in pain and you feel like everything has been taken from you. That’s how they want you to feel, and that’s how they want you to react. We have to fight back, but prove there’s a better way than coldly killing.” I stroked her hair as she settled back against my chest, “Doc wouldn’t have wanted to spill more blood in his name.”

Adrienne nodded silently, another wave of grief overcame her and she collapsed further against me, eyes closed. I held her quietly, staring out of the window as the country whipped past far below.

Chapter Thirty-Three

It was the middle of the night by the time the helicopter began its descent. The helipad rushed up to greet us as we came into land, the floodlights illuminating the large 'H' on the concrete that was surrounded by a large field, sprawling off into the night's inky darkness. A small group stood behind the steps away from the downdraft of the blades as we touched down with a gentle bump.

Adrienne had been sleeping for the majority of the flight. Groggily she stirred, pushing the blanket off herself and looked around. The whirr of the rotors began to die off as one of the welcoming party approached. Tall, thin, with a slender fit suit tailored around him, he wrenched the door open and beckoned us out. "Come with us Mr Wolf, Ms A." We cautiously followed him from the haven of the helicopter. The chilly night air whistled around the exposed landing pad, brusquely shaking us awake. The cooling breeze filled my lungs. I took a deep, greedy breath of it, drinking it in. It soothed the spinning in my head and I exhaled slowly. "*What do I do now?*" I asked, staring upwards, hoping for some sort of divine answer.

The stars were solemn in their celestial silence.

The breath gave me time to clear my head. I hurried forward to catch up with Adrienne and this new stranger who had continued to walk into the night as I had stopped to collect my thoughts.

"We have to act now," Adrienne was speaking, "Goulder's death and implementation of their plan means we're all likely to be hunted down as soon as the Phoenix's new ComChip goes live."

The man walked alongside her, silent, head bowed in thought. From what I could make out in the darkness he was tall, slender, with a pointed chin that he stroked with a long finger whilst deep in contemplation. Eventually he spoke, voice deep and clear, "I understand your need to mobilise Miss A, and that we're all running out of time but–"

I cut across him, forcefully. "With all due respect, sir, there are no 'buts' here," the clear night's air had given me a renewed energy, "if we sit and speculate and give ourselves more things to consider, we give them too much time. They already have an overwhelming advantage. Surprise may be our only option."

The man turned to face me, a smile creeping across his thin lips. He had been military at some point in his life. The way he carried himself, standing upright with his hands behind his back as he walked. "As you say, Mr Wolf," he stared me up and down, "but," he bit on the final letter, emphasising how he felt about my interruption, "we have been working to disrupt them for a while and we have to ensure that the time to strike is right. Miss A has been feeding us information anything we could make use of, their computer schematics, personnel files, ways to disrupt the launch of the new ComChip before tomorrow. We do not have the luxury of a second chance."

A rush of excitement warmed me against the midnight chill. There was hope. A tiny spark we could nurture, breathe life into, and use to light the touch paper of a fightback. The walk through the forest passed quickly after that. The excitement pushing me on, following in the footsteps of Adrienne and the military man who had gone ahead, speaking in hushed whispers. Eventually, just as dawn was breaking we reached an old manor house, the gravel drive swept across the front, stones kissed by the sun's early rays. The building itself was old but well maintained, with the stately grandeur of a bygone age. The sunrise behind it silhouetted the chimneys, triangular roofs and rounded towers against the pink and orange hues, making the edifice even more imposing as we approached. The light crept slowly over the cracked tiles, I stood there, watching the sun's processional march upward until the first rays began to caress my forehead. There was a crisp chill in the air, but the sun's warmth was comforting against it. Adrienne and the military man stood in the arched doorway. I took one final breath of the crisp morning air and stepped inside.

Chapter Thirty-Four

The smell of damp clung to every drape and carpet in the dingy hallway. We stepped forward into the gloom, ageing floorboards creaking underfoot. Our slender guide ushered us into a room off the main entranceway. The room we found ourselves in was a complete departure from the aestheticism and grandeur of the façade. It was cold and clinical; the bare concrete walls had been painted a brilliant white, which the years had turned to a murky grey. Green enamel lamps hung from the ceiling, with dust dancing beneath their beams. Computers were banked against the walls, humming electrically and contributing to the warmth of the room. A projector flickered through graphs and numbers as well as a map of the world onto the wall at the far end.

A gaggle of people crowded beneath it, staring up avidly. The nerves were palpable as we approached. Adrienne and I stood towards the back of the group, watching what appeared to be a countdown progress, second by second, almost in time with my heartbeats. I was acutely aware of them now, each one ticking past, thumping away in my chest. The military man stepped in front of the crowd and cleared his throat.

"Ladies and gentlemen," he began, "it's time."

There was a sharp intake of collective breath. A low hum of nervous voices began to spread through the crowd. The military man nodded and gestured for their babble to end as he continued.

"We are in the presence of Michael Wolf. Finally, the last stage of our plan can come to fruition. We know that Prime Minister Wyndham is going to make his announcement at midday; this gives us time to prepare."

I frowned. Prepare for what? How are these people, huddled in a concrete room, staring at a wall going to compete with Wyndham, the Phoenix and the brainwashed millions who are going to be swarming after them come midday?

The military man caught my eye, seeing me frown. He turned back to his crowd and began to bark instructions. "You three, set up the room, you two begin the process of getting into the ComChip's communication setups so we'll be ready to broadcast as soon as possible. You four, ensure that we can get across the signal of Wyndham's announcement with our own, everything has to run like clockwork."

The huddled mass began to disband, a couple remained, monitoring the projections on the screen. The banks of computers were busied as several technicians typed frantically, the screens flicking from data screens to timers and a large green line which jumped haphazardly up and down across the screen. The military man glided effortlessly over to me, placed his hand on my shoulder and guided me towards the door again.

"Come with me Mr Wolf, we have a lot to do." His voice was cajoling but firm, it was encouragement but without the option of refusal.

When we made it back to the corridor, I cleared my throat.

“What are we doing here?” I said, keeping pace with his longer strides.

He smiled a thin, knowing smile, looking sideways at me. “We are here at Bletchley Park, the secret base for Britain’s wartime decoding operation, to launch a fight back against the Phoenix.” His voice quivered with an excitement which didn’t befit his military background. He recovered his composure and spoke again. “My name is Captain Richard Terry, I was in the army for twenty-five years, serving in conflicts all around the world. That is,” he hesitated, sizing me up before continuing, “until I was approached by a man in a suit, in my command tent in Bolivia.” He carried on his story, hands behind his back, head slightly bowed, “He didn’t give a name, just told me that any prisoners we had had been signed over to his people. He gave me a slip of paper with an official seal and a *top secret* stamp and that was that.” He paused, the memory was obviously causing him difficulty. “I couldn’t just leave it alone. I had taken orders before, without question, for most of my life. This was different. The whole situation didn’t make sense. I tried to chase it up with my superiors, all of whom were all very opaque with their answers. I was even told to stop chasing this, to let the prisoners go, that they weren’t worth the cost of keeping them and the representative had bought them as well as some of the officers’ silences. I saw the transporters arrive a couple of days later, heavily armed mercenaries, a black truck, no insignias, nothing. They were beating some of the prisoners, herding them all to the back of their truck. One of the prisoners made a break for it, but was cut down by one of the guards.” His eyes shone with anger and sadness. He was reliving the experience and it was written all over his face. “They were young; we’d had to take them in after they had been recruited as child soldiers for a local militia." He sighed heavily. "I stormed into my superior's tent, full of anger, about to shake the answers out of him, but there wasn't anyone there. Just a file on a desk."

"What happened next?" I coaxed, we were reaching a small doorway at the left near the end of a corridor.

Terry looked me up and down, halted for a second and continued, "I found out who was behind the prisoner transfer, and what they were going to do with them. It was the Phoenix, they were going to take them to their research facility and use them for experiments," he shuddered. "Some were to do with the mind, how it worked, how to judge the mental strength of the subjects, in short, torture. Others, they were going to kill, but not before turning them into half man, half cybernetic warriors, twisted and broken." He shook his head as though trying to dislodge the memories from behind his eyes. "I ran. I was so ashamed of running, but I was more ashamed that I hadn't fought harder to try and save them."

I nodded, suddenly I saw Terry without his army breeding. He was just a man, grey and tired, even though his posture was straight and tall he seemed smaller, as though the weight of his ghosts were pushing on his shoulders. I reached out and patted him on the back.

"We all have ghosts, Richard," I told him, looking back down the corridor. For a second I could have sworn I saw Doc, Mark, Katherine and Jeanette linger far behind us. The sadness in their eyes made me turn away. I looked back at Terry, "We're here because of them, fighting because we still believe that they shouldn't die for nothing."

He smiled back at me. The relief seemed to flow through him, as if my consolation was absolution. We stepped over the threshold and into the smaller room. A spotlight hung from the centre of the ceiling. A black sheet had been stretched over the far wall, a video camera on a tripod stood alone in the middle.

Chapter Thirty-Five

Captain Terry stood inside the room, his cropped greying hair grazed the low ceiling. He gestured to the wooden stool in front of the crude dark backdrop. I tentatively followed. I hovered next to the vacant stool, reluctant to take the seat.

"What are we doing here?" I asked. The nerves made my voice creak ever so slightly.

Terry smiled, "Nothing to worry about Mr Wolf, we merely brought you here to record a message. A message which we will play at the same time as Wyndham makes his announcement to the country. We'll broadcast it around the world, as we have it on good authority that the Phoenix's representatives are all in position to become commanders of their provinces when the upgraded ComChip goes online. We will infiltrate the signal and try to stop as many people as possible from hearing his message."

I smiled, elated. The plan was simple, efficient and very clever. The only way to begin a fight back was to beat the Phoenix at their own game. We needed a way to get into people's homes, to try and awaken them to their situation, and the same system the Phoenix used couldn't be more perfect for the task. A flurry of questions flew up into my head, a couple made it out of my mouth before I could stop them.

"If they find us, what will they do?" The nerves were raising my heartbeat. I paced across the bare concrete.

Captain Terry shrugged, "They'll try to kill us."

"And if we don't?"

"They'll try to kill us."

I chuckled, "Ok, I can't say that's entirely new." I sighed, "Fuck it. Bring it on." My words were as much to build my own confidence as to instil it in the others milling around me.

"What happens when the people see the message? I mean, they saw the Prime Minister killed on TV the day of Wyndham's coup and there was no response, no riots, nothing, not even an official response, it just happened. So what chance do we have?" The next question leapt out as quickly as the first. "They didn't join us before, why would they now?"

The captain smiled. "When the coup happened the Phoenix used the ComChip to subdue the people. Like mental anaesthetic. The people watched on, swallowing the terror before them, accepting of everything. No will or power to fight or try to stand up against them. *We're* going to use the ComChip this time. We may just be able to get some people over to our side." He picked up a sheaf of papers from the desk on the far side of the room and pointed to the camera. "We have a developed a script we would like you to read into the camera, ready for the broadcast."

I took the script from him, and looked down. It was atrocious. The message didn't have any guts, any drive at all. I shook my head, trying to stifle a short snort of laughter. I looked up from the nonsensical scrawling at Captain Terry. "We're not giving them anything here.

No options, no hope, nothing. Why should people desert their comforts to join us if we don't offer them anything new? If we don't make them realise how badly they need this, as well as we need them, they won't come." I waved the paper in his face. "We have to give them more, or the belief of more, otherwise people will never change."

Captain Terry looked from me to the script, and then back to me. His thin brows furrowed over his stern eyes. "Ok. Well, I'll leave it with you." He walked over to behind the camera and gestured to the stool in front of it.

I stayed where I was standing, took a deep breath and composed my thoughts before sitting on the cold, wooden stool. The spotlight above me made it difficult to see beyond a few metres ahead of me. The tiny red light of the camera concentrated its glare on me. I took a final deep breath and stared back, knowing there were people behind the lens. The expectancy was tangible, the nervous energy flooded into the room.

"My name is Michael Wolf." I began hesitantly. "I was the founder of the Phoenix technologies corporation and I need to tell you that the life that they have built for you is not what I had intended. The Phoenix was taken over from the inside, by an insidious group of people who saw the products we were creating and saw an opportunity. The opportunity to exploit you." I pointed down the lens. "They took away what made you the individual. They made you turn a blind eye to the famines, the wars and the poverty. They needed you docile. They need you contained and helpless, because it helps them to exercise control. No-one would dare to oppose them; anyone who did was eliminated brutally. I know that's hard to believe, but I have seen it. I have felt the blood of friends on my hands as they died in my arms. They killed a few to make a point, some just because they could. Others they killed as experiments. After today, with the upgraded ComChip, you, the people will submit to their control completely. You will be herded and dictated to directly. You will not question them, defy them or even be able to create your own opinions. You will cohabit with your families but you will not see them, you will not have any emotional attachments. Your children will be brought up and indoctrinated into their organisation and in all too few generations, all humanity will be wiped from the world. It will not, in any way, be a fresh start. All human life will be condensed down into mere servitude. You will be born. You will exist. You will consume. And you will die."

I let the silence hang heavy in the room for a moment.

"I am so sorry. I have to take the blame for allowing someone I trusted to turn on me. They saw the money before the human value. He removed me from my organisation and sold it to governments, militias and corporations. People who saw the technological advances we had made as solely profit-making tools for the control of you. There is responsibility on my side. That is why I am here, trying to rally support for the fight against them. I can't do it alone. There is so much that we as people can do when we band together. The Phoenix know this, they are scared of this fact. Please. For everyone we have lost, for everything we stand to lose, stand with us and take back our future. We are stronger together, and when we unite we can achieve so much. Look at the cities around you. Look at the moon and know there are footprints there! If there is anything that can convince you to back us, look at your families.

Really look at them. I have said a lot, and not a lot can convince you to defend yourself. But when you look around at families, friends and lovers, you will realise that you have a lot more to lose than you think."

Another pause. Another silence.

"You didn't fall in love with them because they're the same as you, you didn't perpetuate the human race to create clones of yourselves. Individuality is what makes the human race so phenomenal. Instead of upgrading the ComChip and submitting to Wyndham and the Phoenix forever, stand with us. I'm not asking you to believe in us; trust me I don't have all the answers. But no-one does, don't be paralysed by the fear of not knowing. The future is worth the risk. We can build, thrive and learn from each other. Fight with us. Thank you."

The red light blinked off. There was a second's pause before Captain Terry was at my side, he clapped me on the back and smiled. "You were right, that was better than the script."

Chapter Thirty-Six

I left the filming room allowing the relief to flood over me. For the first time in months I had been able to take the initiative, stand up and fight. I bounced along the musty corridor. The grandfather clock in the hallway was approaching nine. Three hours, only three hours before all hell could possibly break loose. The damp air was cloying in my throat. I coughed twice as some of the thick dust kicked up from the carpet. Sneezing violently I blundered towards the back door and, with some friendly directions from a chuckling engineer, I made my way out towards the gardens.

The fresh air streamed into my lungs, refreshing and crisp. I drank it in. The deep soothing breaths comforted me as I wandered aimlessly through the immaculately manicured grounds. My rambling eventually led me to the banks of a pond, the fountain sprung out of the middle. I sat on the damp grass, staring into the dark waters. The twisting in my stomach was back. I didn't feel alone. The memories of Katherine, Mark, Jeanette and Doc hung around my head, each final death mask frozen in front of my eyes. I bowed my head. Warm tears began to make tracks from the corners of my eyes, trickling their way over and around the scrapes and scars which had become etched into my face. I hadn't had a chance to grieve for any of them, the speed of events had kept me going until now, a strange blend of adrenaline and fear had been driving me forward, without time to stop and take in the enormity of what was happening.

I wiped the tears away. They were useless; they couldn't bring any of them back, the only choice was onwards. The realisation of what we were trying to set in motion hit me, it was a total revolution. If people began to join us, the change would be immediate, there would be no more need for pretence from the Phoenix. They would come after us with everything they had in their diabolical arsenal with unimaginable brutality. I felt sure that there were things I hadn't seen yet, I remembered the covered domes that the drones had been working on the first time I had encountered Joe and his area of the Phoenix's organisation. They had crackled with electricity and whirred as their motors had ominously begun to spin. I had seen the insanity set into Joe, and the way he acted without mercy, yet the unknown was still more terrifying to me.

The pack of cigarettes landed lightly in my lap. I craned my neck around to see who had dropped them. Adrienne flopped down onto the grass beside me, leaning back on her hands and stretching her legs out. She smiled as the mid-morning sunlight bathed her. I toyed with the rectangular cardboard case flicking it between my hands. The large silver "V" with the word "Victory" caught the sunlight and glittered. It had been months since my last cigarette and somehow I didn't feel like a smoke right now.

"Where did you find these?" I asked, waving the cigarettes at Adrienne.

"One of the storerooms here," she said, "looks like they were left over from the eighties."

I nodded and looked away, back over the pond.

"We're going to war, aren't we Dad?" Adrienne was nervous. It was strange, her calmness had been a grounding influence. When I had been shot, she looked after me along with Doc with a steadying serenity.

I sighed, "It looks that way. I don't know how this will play out, the changes are so huge, we can't possibly know what will happen. One thing's for sure though," I paused, looking back at Adrienne, "the Phoenix won't give up their control without a fight."

Adrienne nodded, agreeing silently. Her eyes swept away over the pond, a silent sadness seemed to hang around her. I realised that she must have felt the same way I did when she came out here, the first real opportunity to grieve for people she had lost. She'd loved Doc, the same way he had loved her. I reached out, desperately trying to console her, knowing I couldn't do it with words. She leant over, resting her head on my shoulder.

We sat in the stillness of our silent grief for what felt like hours. The only sounds were the whisper of the wind through the trees and the soft splashes of the fountain. A ringing phone interrupted the tranquil silence. Adrienne answered, nodding silently. She hung up without saying a word, sat up and turned to face me. There was a jittery excitement flickering in her eyes. "It's time." She leapt off the grass and gracefully glided back towards the house.

I took a long, lingering look back across the water, out over to the trees, trying to savour a final moment of stillness. I left the scarlet packet of cigarettes in the grass and followed Adrienne back into the eye of the storm.

Chapter Thirty-Seven

The room we had been led to when we first arrived was humming with activity. More people had arrived, flitting around the room, taking nervous glances up towards the projections on the bare concrete walls. Captain Terry paced nervously along the far side where the computers were being hurriedly prepared. He chewed at his bottom lip nervously, perfectly straight teeth leaving whitened marks. The thick sense of anticipation and fear hung above the room. The ancient metal clock ticked down, approaching the midday deadline. The tense feeling snaked through my stomach, tying it in tight knots. The unsettling knowledge that we were about to go into battle rushed towards me, making my head spin. I wished I hadn't left the cigarettes in the grass. I tapped nervously against my thigh, trying to calm myself.

Captain Terry sidled up and stood beside me. "Are you ready?" he asked, voice controlled, but barely audible above the hive of activity around us.

I shrugged, surveying the bustling scene unfold. "Are you?"

He snorted a short burst of tetchy laughter, "I suppose not."

I looked him up and down, his tall, slender frame not betraying the myriad of emotions within. His military breeding helped hold his external calm. I glanced back to the clock, the relentless procession of time dragging us all inexorably towards the point of no return. One minute remained. The silence swept through the room in an instant, holding its collective breath as the clock swept close to midday.

"Ten, nine, eight, seven," the countdown began. A voice from the other side of the room called out through the silence. A final flurry of activity as the banks of computers went through their final checks, preparing to begin, "four, three, two, one. We are live." The clock struck midday. All eyes turned towards the projector. The figures and maps that had been scrolling along for the past few hours had been replaced by a single split screen. On the left, Wyndham's prime ministerial plinth had been prepared. He strolled up to the podium, the confidence exuding from him as he fixed the room and the camera with a discomforting smile. His cool eyes swept over the journalists before he fixed them firmly onto the barrel of the lens.

On the right, our message was being prepared. As Wyndham began to speak about progress and unity, our video began to play. The wall of computer screens on the far wall burst into life, one of the technicians called across that we were online and the signal was good. A sense of relief seemed to lighten the mood around the room. Our message was being fired out there, right into the ComChips of the people watching the official announcement. The broadcasts were now in full swing, Wyndham burbled through a long list of Phoenix propaganda about peace through strength and uniformity, while I was approaching my apology for the savagery I had inadvertently created.

As Wyndham's message finished, he raised a hand in a triumphalist salute, bathing in the applause of the adoring crowd. Instead of journalists with prying questions the stately wood panelled room had been packed with a crowd of people who I assumed had been rounded up from the public in order to play the part of the adoring faithful.

"How do we know if the people heard us?" I turned away from the screen to face Captain Terry.

He shrugged, smiled and clapped me on the back, "We don't really. We've done everything we can. All we can do now is wait."

I sank onto a bench next to the doorway, all the waiting was crippling. Wyndham's voice peeled across the room from the projector screen. "Do you really think we didn't know what you were doing, Mr Wolf? After everything we have shown you so far you really think that we could be hacked so easily without our knowledge?" He laughed. The cold and clear sound rang out over the room. "Thank you. Thank you for giving us the exact location of your pathetic little band of brothers. We will eradicate you all. Before the day is out you will be barely a memory in our glorious victory. Your names will be forgotten, your families destroyed, anyone who swears you existed will face the same fate as you."

I moved from my seat on the wall into the centre of the room. Wyndham's face loomed above me, projected high onto the wall, so huge I could see the spittle begin to creep out of the corner of his mouth. I felt sure he couldn't hear me, and I didn't have anything to say to him either. Instead I turned my attention to the room. Panic had begun to set in, the roar of feverish conversation drowned out Wyndham's speech. I pulled the plug from the projector and Wyndham disappeared instantly.

I climbed onto a chair and stared around. Some people were standing, dumbstruck, the total terror etched into every line on their faces. Others were crying, shaking and staring around in the desperate hope of comfort. A few were making for the door, heads down in the hope of being unnoticed. "OK," I began, my voice nowhere near loud enough to clear the din. I raised it and tried again. "OK." Silence followed.

All eyes were fixed on me, the tension crackled electrically. "Now we know what we're facing. The next few hours, days, months, hell, maybe even years will be hard. We need to fight, now more than ever. If you want to leave, go now, no-one will stop you. Maybe the Phoenix will accept your surrender." I shrugged, "But maybe they think you have information they can extract from you. Do you know who they are? Do you really think they'll be forgiving enough to just let you walk away from everything?"

The few in the doorway hesitated, the rest of the room's attention flicked from them back to me. The clamour for the exit ceased, as the realisation of what I was saying sank in.

"If they come here, we're dead!" someone called out, terrified.

"If we don't try and fight them we're dead anyway," I said. "Isn't it better to have died for something than to have lived for nothing? What we're doing here could be the start of a brilliant future. Do you have children?" I scanned the room, a few were nodding, a few others were crying at the thought of their families. "If you don't want to defend yourselves, defend them. Defend their right to be individuals, to mess up, to find someone who turns their world upside down. There is so much worth protecting. Don't tell me you're going to walk away from that."

"He's right," a soft voice called out. I looked around to see a tiny woman sitting on a table near the screens. Her legs dangled in the air as she spoke. She stared back at me; her chestnut brown eyes peered out from beneath a jet black fringe. "But we're not fighters, Mr Wolf, we're unarmed and scared."

I stepped off the chair and ambled over to her. "I know. I'm not a fighter either, this fight chose me. Trust me, if I hadn't ever noticed my ComChip and tried to remove it I wouldn't be here now." I shrugged, "But I am. And even though I'm not a fighter I believe in what we're doing, and what we can do, together."

She smiled, the strength of her conviction was returning to her. She gracefully leapt off the bench and turned to face the room. She was barely five feet tall and extremely slight. I was sure if she had turned sideways, she would've disappeared. "Fuck it." The two words took me aback, I glanced down at her. "We can't just roll over, otherwise all this," she waved around the room we stood in, "would be for nothing, we all came here to try and build something better, so let's finish it!"

The roar that greeted her words was astounding, a mixture between laughter and cheering. Suddenly the room burst back into life, Captain Terry was barking instructions, directing the technicians and engineers to their various roles. I glanced over to Adrienne, she was occupied with assembling her utility belt, knives, grenades and pistols hung in their holsters as she strapped it around her waist. Two long narrow swords hung at her back on bandoliers which crossed on her chest. It felt strange to be standing still in the middle of this melee, everyone was preparing for a fight, but no-one knew what the next move was going to be. I made my way out of the room, needing to get some air. I picked up a heavy black pistol from a nearby table, checked it was loaded, tucked it into the back of my trousers and headed for the door. The sound of the commotion became more distant as I headed towards the front door.

I stepped out onto the porch and froze. Wyndham was standing on the grass. He had not come alone.

Chapter Thirty-Eight

The iron sky framed the scene, Wyndham and two armed guards stood on the grass, staring straight at me. They were flanked and followed by a large crowd stretching back as far as I could see. Men, women and children, all dishevelled and with the same vacant look in their eyes stood silently. They were mixed in with other armed guards, who were milling around. They had dispersed themselves evenly with the civilians, making it harder to target them and not hit the innocents who were present, but only physically. The ComChip upgrade had begun. Wyndham had his drones, and he had brought the fight to us.

My hand reached for the gun at my back, I grasped it firmly, the tacky rubber reassuring in my palm.

"Mr Wolf," Wyndham said smiling, arms outstretched, "welcome to the future! Don't they all look magnificent?"

I stared around at the faces of the people behind him, blank and emotionless. Looking closer, some of them had been amalgamated with pieces of metal, some with limbs removed to make way for weaponry or carbon fibre legs. The cybernetic soldiers that Captain Terry had seen plans for in the Bolivian jungle were here, in front of me. The horror shortened my breaths. Nausea swam in the back of my throat. I choked on the lump it had caused.

"It's not the word I would have chosen, Wyndham," I called back, ensuring I spoke loudly enough to be heard inside. My heart began to beat faster, thumping against the inside of my breastbone and pushing the lump in my throat further upwards. I gripped onto the gun tighter, fingernails biting into my hand. I pulled it from my waistband and raised it. I was greeted by a clatter of rifles being raised. A human barrier of drones snapped to attention, blocking my path to Wyndham. His laughter carried over from the middle of his huddle.

"I don't care if you're not impressed, Michael," he said, "I am, and the fact of the matter is, even if you kill me, everyone around me will tear you apart on command, with their bare hands if needs be."

My arm didn't waver, I wasn't afraid of the drones. The ones who were still just ordinary people, they were so innocent in all of this, just chess pieces on the board that Wyndham, Joe and I had created.

I pulled the hammer back, hearing the click as it locked, ready to fire.

Behind me, the door swung open, Adrienne was alongside me in an instant, AR-15 in hand. Captain Terry followed her swiftly out, freezing as he saw Wyndham.

"Ah, Captain," Wyndham called, "it's been a long time since Bolivia."

I hesitated, "You *know* him?"

Terry nodded, "I didn't want to tell you before, but he was the one who came to me in Bolivia, he gave the order for the guard to shoot that boy. It's been a long time, and I never thought I'd be this close to him again."

I glanced away from Wyndham's security detail to the Captain who stood calm, revolver in hand. "Are you OK here?" I asked.

Terry nodded, his jaw was clenched, a small vein had begun to throb at his temple.

Above us the windows of the towers were flung open, our group were leaning out. All the guns we had were pointed towards the crowd of invaders on our front lawn. Adrienne whispered in my ear, "It's OK Dad, I've been in contact with the Alpha squad, they'll be here soon. All we need to do is hold them off until back-up arrives."

The silent standoff began, both sides unwilling to strike first. Above us in one of the towers a nervy technician fiddled with his rifle. His fingers shook as he raised it to his shoulder, staring down the sight. The sweat made his fingers slick, he fumbled for grip. He failed.

The single shot rang out through the silence. The bullet whipped through the air and struck one of the drones close to Wyndham. His blood spattered over the immaculately suited Prime Minister and his guards, all of whom stood motionless as the body dropped to the floor in front of him.

Another silence followed. Adrienne, Captain Terry and I exchanged worried looks. Wyndham looked to his left, gave a sharp, swift nod and took two steps backwards before retreating behind the tree line. The guard fiddled with a cuff on his uniform, pressing buttons hastily before straightening up, raising his machine gun and firing up towards the window our initial bullet had come from.

The drones and cybernetic soldiers began to advance, slowly at first before breaking into a sprint. Gunfire began to clatter around us, a hail of bullets whipped through the air, cracking roof tiles and shattering windows. The drones were upon Adrienne, Terry and me in an instant. They clawed at our faces and bodies, frenzied and out of control. I fired into the crowd, indiscriminately. I couple of the drones fell. I prayed I hadn't hit a child. Wave after wave of attack battered against us. It was a bruising, draining fight. In the melee I dropped my gun. I resorted to punching wildly at the seemingly unending attackers. My knuckles were bloody and swollen, I was convinced I had broken a hand, but had no option but to continue pushing forward. I charged outward, shoving drones out of my way. I looked back to where Adrienne had drawn a knife and was slashing at the onrushing hoard. I looked around for Captain Terry but he had been dragged out of sight. The suffocating roar, the heat and the weight of the bodies around us had made it hard to breathe in the crush.

I made it out behind the first wave of onrushing cyborgs and looked back at the building. Fire had begun to curl over the roof, smoking steadily as more bullets and grenades were being exchanged between the soldiers below and our bunch of fighters. The smell of fire became stronger as the smoke began to plume over the battlefield and up into the grey sky. Explosions rocked the building, sending bricks, glass and broken bodies flying through the air above me. Adrienne appeared next to me, panting heavily. Her face was streaked with blood and dirt, she had been beaten and bloodied. She bent over, hands on her knees sucking in as much air as she could.

"Terry?" I yelled over the gunfire and explosions.

She looked up at me, and shook her head. "I couldn't see him."

I nodded, resting a hand gently on her back. "Come on, we need to get to Wyndham before he gets away." She straightened up, nodded and ran off into the trees. I took a quick look back to the house, its proud façade pockmarked by a hail of bullets. The cyborgs had begun to swarm over the walls and through the holes in the ceiling, undeterred by the flames lapping around them. They reached through the windows and hurled the battling guards from them. I turned away and chased after Adrienne into the forest.

The rain had begun to fall, the drops rattling against the leaves, the scent of damp earth kicked up as we hurtled further in. Adrienne stopped every few metres, stooping to track Wyndham's footprints before sweeping on, further into the dark. I carried on, following her to a clearing. Just as I broke past the treeline a pair of gunshots cracked out like a whip. I stopped suddenly, skidding on the wet ground. I looked down, patting my chest. I hadn't been shot. But then–

Adrienne.

She stood two metres ahead of me, too still. Incredibly slowly, she began to sink to her knees. I lurched forward, sliding on the mud and caught her before she fell completely. She looked at me, the wide eyed terror on her face, breaths shallow and sharp. "Dad," she started, the blood had begun to trickle out of the corner of her mouth, "Dad, I'm scared."

"It's ok, sweetheart," I cradled her close, clutching her head to my chest, "it's ok, don't be scared, we're going to make you better, the Alpha squad are coming."

Wyndham laughed, "No they're not, you're alone here, and your daughter's going to die."

I stared at him, transfixed by his maleficence. "You bastard! You murdering, spineless, sack of shit!" I screamed. The rain had begun to come down even harder, cutting my face and covering the tears which had begun to burn my eyes. The spit flew from my lips as I bellowed above the battle and the raging wind.

"It's ok, everything's ok," I whispered to Adrienne cradling her close, willing her to live. Her breaths had become ragged, the coarse rattle of death dogging each one of them. Her eyes stayed shut. I clung to her, hoping against hope I'd see her open them again. The bubbling blood ran down her cheek and began to drip into the mud at my knees.

Wyndham just laughed even more, "Really? Is that the best you have?" He strolled over, pointed Oxfords squelching in the mud. He raised the long barrelled Magnum and lazily clicked the hammer back. "She's dead. You know that by now. Lying to her isn't going to help."

Adrienne had stopped breathing in my arms. I stared down at her, my eyes widened in horror and anguish. The pain tore through me, my ribs felt as though someone was prizing them apart, leaving my heart exposed. A grieved shriek escaped from me. My head craned back, the rain pounding on my face, filling my eyes and stinging my cheeks.

I wiped away the water which had filled my vision and found myself confronted with the opaque barrel of Wyndham's pistol. I reached for the swords hanging behind Adrienne's back, stared up at Wyndham, he was savouring the moment, drinking in the grief that seemed to fuel him. I seized upon his moment of triumphalism and swung the sword from the sheath. The thin sliver of silvery steel flashed through the rain and carved Wyndham's pistol hand from his wrist with the merest of resistance, turning the air around it momentarily red. The

Magnum landed in the dirt with a splat, sending muddy water spattering in droplets onto Adrienne's deathly pale face.

Wyndham screamed in agony, clutching the stump of his arm which was spurting arterial blood. I slowly got to my feet, sliding slightly in the mud. The sword's silver blade shimmered with crimson and crystalline droplets.

He sank to his knees, whimpering softly. The colour was draining from his face as the blood oozed out, mingling with the mud around him. I raised the sword high above my head, staring down at his shaking frame. My breaths were hard and fast, my head throbbed with angry power. The fury was all-consuming, so strong I was paralysed by it. We were both there, in that clearing, staring at one another. The wind whipped around us, blowing rain straight into my face. I squinted through it, my breaths condensing in the cold air. I had reached the point Joe had taunted me with, the moment a person breaks. I screamed an unearthly, agonised bellow. Just as I was about to bring the sword down on Wyndham's neck his eyes rolled backwards, and he slumped, face forwards into the mud.

I froze. My moment had been taken from me by Wyndham's blood loss. I just stood there, staring, wild eyed at his unmoving body. My arms shook, the sword wasn't heavy but suddenly I couldn't keep it in my grasp. It fell from my hands and dug into the soft ground, quivering on its point. I slid over to Adrienne's still body and sank to my knees next to it. I put my hand on her stomach, covering the wound. I was crying again. The hot tears mixed with the cold rain and bathed my cheeks.

"I'm sorry, Adrienne, I'm so so sorry." The words were hollow and quiet between heavy sobs. "I wish I could have protected you, I should have protected you. It should be me lying there. Not you." I kissed her cold forehead, the mud and blood spatters were rough under my lips.

A twig cracked in the trees behind me. It sharpened me, the shaking stopped. I ran to where Wyndham's magnum had landed, still in his severed hand. I prized it out of it and ran away from the sound of squelching footsteps approaching. I hid behind the treeline and watched the owners of the footsteps arrive in the clearing. They strolled over to Wyndham's body, crouched beside it and beckoned to their accomplices. Four guards jogged into the clearing, two lifted Wyndham under his arms and carried him away. The others followed the first man, a spectral shadowy figure, over to Adrienne. He looked down at her, gave her a disinterested poke with the tip of his shoe and nodded to the guards who lifted her in the same way as Wyndham and followed their colleagues from the clearing.

I watched on, horrified. What if Adrienne was still alive? Why didn't I shoot Wyndham, just to make sure? As the tall, grey man turned and walked away, I swallowed the burning vomit to try and stay silent. He took one final squelching walk around the perimeter of the clearing, barely metres from me. I could have sworn we made eye contact for a split second, before he turned away and trudged after the guards who had accompanied him.

I waited for as long as I could, until the strain of the vomit pushing hard against my cheeks and through my throat became too much. I opened my mouth and relented to the burning.

Chapter Thirty-Nine

The smoke from the smouldering ruins of the house swept out over the battlefield, curling upward round the branches of the trees which stood, resolute and silent around the edge of the scorched earth. I stumbled forward, wiping the spittle and vomit from my chin. The once pristine grass had been chewed up and smeared with mud and blood from the short but violent conflict that had ensued in our absence. Bodies from both sides were strewn among the chunks of rubble flung from the explosions that tore the house before me apart. The once tall and elegant towers and pointed rooftops had been pulled apart. Jagged holes had been torn out of the façade where the cyborgs had flung tiles from their positions and crawled through to eliminate our band of volunteers. Smoke billowed up through the gaps in the rooftops, as if the whole building was suffocating on its final smoky breaths. I felt a pang of fear in my stomach as I stared at the scene. I ran through the body strewn field, over to the porch where Captain Terry, Adrienne and I had been when the horde had attacked.

The footprints on the wooden floor were so close together from the stampede they had all blurred into one muddy carpet. Captain Terry's body lay in the middle of them, battered and broken. The horde had torn into him, they had been unarmed and their attack had been brutal. Bloody scratches were carved into his skin, large purple and black bruises had swollen his face to three times the size it had been. All his teeth had been broken, several of them littered the bloody pool around his head and there were footprints all over his torso where the drones had trampled him after he had fallen.

I stared at him for what felt like an age, another victim of this brutal war the Phoenix had started in their quest for complete dominance. The anger swelled in my chest and pushed me on, past his corpse and into the steadily smoking remains of the main building. More bodies were littered all over the hallway, barely visible through the plumes of smoke which hung in the air. I coughed, covered my mouth and pushed further on, hoping desperately to find any survivors within the wreckage. As I made it to the centre of the hallway a firm and desperate grip on my ankle made me jump with shock. I stared through the smoke at the petite hand, reaching out from beneath a bullet ridden corpse. I pushed the body off the owner of the hand and hauled her to her feet. She stared, wide eyed with terror. I took her hand and pulled her out of the door. We made it to the side of the building and stopped, taking deep and long breaths of the cool air, spluttering as we rid the smoke from our lungs.

"What's your name?" I said between coughs.

"Sarah, Mr Wolf," she wheezed back, "Sarah. Have you seen Captain Terry, Adrienne, anyone?" she stared at me, eyes wide with hope.

I looked back at her, downcast and shook my head. "They didn't make it." I could feel the tears begin to sting the corners of my eyes. I didn't even know why the shadowy figure in the clearing had taken Adrienne, whether she was still alive, whether Wyndham had survived. I slumped back against the wall. The warmth of the steadily burning fire warmed my back through the bricks.

I looked up at Sarah, she was short, shapely, with chocolate brown hair. Her attractive face was smeared with blood and grime. Her dark brown eyes looked me up and down, waiting for me to make the next move.

"What happened in there?" I asked, the smoke had made my throat sting and my voice croak, "After I followed Adrienne through to the clearing?"

Sarah bent over, hands on her knees. She shook her head. "We were overrun. It's as simple as that, they were all over us before we knew. We weren't soldiers. They just tore through the building like it wasn't there. We were OK until they started climbing through the windows and through the ceilings, the panic spread faster than the fire. They were coming at us from all sides, half machine, half men, people were running, they caught them, they…" she trailed off, the horror of reliving the slaughter plain to see. "I hid, a body fell on top of me and I just lay there, trying to stay still, hoping they didn't find me." Sarah began to cry, wiping the silent tears away from her dirtied face.

I struggled to my feet, shoes sliding in the mud. I reached out and rubbed Sarah's back. "You did what you could, Sarah, we weren't prepared for them, what they could – what they were willing to do."

Sarah looked up at me, nodded and sniffed back the tears. "I'm sorry Mr Wolf, I can't carry on this fight. Even if they come for me, I need to be back with my family. I have to warn them, to try and get them to safety before the Phoenix takes them away too."

I nodded, sometimes it had been easy to forget that the people around me were all fighting to protect something too. I wrapped Sarah in a hug. "Thank you," I murmured, "You did everything you could have. Please, allow me to take you to where you need to be."

She stepped back from the embrace, smiled and nodded, "Thank you, Mr Wolf, for believing there was something to fight for, something better than the Phoenix."

I shrugged, "You all knew that anyway, that's why you were here."

We stumbled away from the building to the car park, where a selection of vehicles had been abandoned by their owners. I picked a Range Rover, dark and imposing it stood in the corner. It looked as though it had been here the least amount of time. We broke the windows and after fiddling with the wires under the steering wheel for a few minutes the engine burbled into life.

I swung it out of the car park and onto the road. The sun was setting behind the haze of smoke which was still rising from the mangled ruins of Bletchley Park. The wind was whistling through the broken windows. Sarah huddled up in the passenger seat, trying to shield herself from the blustering chill. It was too loud to try and talk, so we passed the hours in silence, Sarah occasionally pointing directions as we approached a town. I recognised it; it had been where I was living before the last few months on the run with Doc and Adrienne. This side of the town was far nicer than where my dingy flat stood.

We slowed outside a suburban semi-detached house, anonymous and uniform. The lights inside glowed invitingly behind the curtains. The street lamps had flickered on and illuminated the patches of concrete pavement beneath them. Sarah took a look up at the house, sighed and turned back to me.

"Thank you, Mr Wolf," she said, smiling weakly, "I hope to see you again sometime, when this has all died down."

"You're welcome Sarah," I returned her smile, "I hope so too."

Slowly she opened her door and stepped out onto the silent street; closed the door with a soft click and scurried up the pathway. Within moments she was inside. The door snapped shut behind her and the security light that had illuminated her steps flickered off. I sat in silence, running my hands over the steering wheel of the Range Rover, the blue glow from the dashboard bathing my hands in a cool hue. I pressed down on the accelerator and the car rolled away from Sarah's house. I made my way across the city. The green spaces became fewer as I approached my old tower block. I parked the car in a tunnel away from the street and darted into the foyer, hoping to stay out of sight. I knew now that the Phoenix had begun enacting their plan. Anyone could be used to spy on anyone else. No-one was safe.

I darted up the stairs, the familiar smell of urine and alcohol mingled oddly comfortingly in my nostrils. My flat was at the end of the corridor, the shabby red door a welcoming sight. I twisted my key in the lock and flopped over the threshold. The door closed behind me, leaving me in the murky gloom of the hallway. Voices were coming from the living room. Slowly, I wandered through the darkness, my footsteps creaking softly on the floorboards beneath the threadbare carpet. The television had switched on by itself. Wyndham was sitting behind a desk, his pale face gaunt and drained. His skin was almost transparent. The lighting had been rigged to make him look as ghostly as possible. His jaw was outlined beneath the pale skin and every sinew could be seen twitching as he sat, waiting to begin speaking. He was alive. The knot in my stomach twisted tight, I reached for the dust covered bottle of whiskey on the table, unscrewed it and took a deep, long draught.

Wyndham had begun to speak, "As some of you know, we, the government face opposition on a daily basis, it is how democracy works." I choked on my drink, stifling a snort of disbelief. Wyndham continued, "However, you, the people should not have to fear the opposition, after all, they are supposed to work with us for the benefit of you. But," he paused, staring straight down the lens of the camera, "there are some that seek to destroy the peace we have brought you. They are dangerous and violent and will not stop. We must act to prevent this. As of tonight there will be patrols on the streets, and a curfew in force. Anyone found to be outside after dark will be presumed to be helping these–" he stopped, toying with the word in order to choose the right one, "terrorists. They will be dealt with accordingly."

The terror froze me to the sofa, the icy chill bit back against the whiskey warmth that had been so soothing to me.

"I know that some of you will be out there, doubting the threat to society these terrorists pose, but please, let this serve as a warning." Wyndham raised the stump of his right arm and brandished it for the camera. "Their leader, Michael Wolf cut my hand off as I was here, handling affairs of state, he would have killed me had it not been for my security team." He waved his stump towards the wall behind him. Out of the shadows,

Adrienne stepped forward. She stood silent at his shoulder, unblinking eyes unwaveringly staring, as if she was seeing inside me.

The breath caught in my chest. I sat silent, stunned. There was a ringing in my ears, as if a gun had gone off in my flat. The dizziness was overwhelming. I slumped onto my side, head resting on the firm cushion of the sofa. I closed my eyes against the horror. Wyndham's voice floated through the darkness. "Wolf and his accomplices had set up base in Bletchley Park, the iconic home of our nation's fightback against tyranny. But when we found them, they destroyed it, burned it to the ground and even killed their own people so they could escape. They scurried back to their dark corners, where we will root them out and terminate them, to keep you safe. Rest assured, no stone will remain unturned until we have made you and your families safe. Anyone with any information is encouraged to come forward. They and their families will be rewarded and protected. You have nothing to fear from us."

I took a deep, long sigh and opened my eyes. The wave of bullshit overcame me, I sat, numb, failing to comprehend what was happening. Wyndham was re-writing history, contorting it to suit his purposes. The control the Phoenix had gained was absolute. There was no safe place, nowhere to run. The message was clear. Wyndham was going to use everything he had at his disposal to hunt me down.

Chapter Forty

The next few days rolled by in a fug of cigarette smoke and whiskey. Days came and went, and every night I watched sleeplessly from the windows as the patrols roamed past the tower block. They were obviously cyborgs, the metallic parts and wiring gleamed when it caught the beams beneath the streetlights. In the early days there were a few stragglers on the streets after dark, but they were soon violently discouraged. Whispers began to spread, rumours of relatives disappearing, being swept up from their homes.

During daylight hours, people began to place posters around the walls of buildings. They gathered to hold vigils at places where the most recent victims of disappearances had lived. All the while I tried to stay off the streets, keeping my face hidden if I did have to venture out.

The posters of the missing were not the only ones that had been appearing. During advert breaks of television shows, government branded messages relayed the information of my pursuit by the Phoenix. Every night the news programmes were filled with more fabricated stories about the destruction the alleged terror groups had committed. Often Wyndham appeared, blaming the disappearances on terrorists. Every time I ventured out I saw fewer people on the streets. A combination of fear and the Phoenix's ComChip kept them inside, away from the truth, away from people who could help them.

Once, a child stared at me as I walked past a playground. I could tell he knew who I was. By the time he had managed to attract the attention of his mother I had run around a corner and out of sight. After that I decided it had become too risky to leave the flat. Every day I wrote what I could remember from the previous months in Mark's battered old notebook, continuing to add his annotations and adding more of my own. I was afraid. I knew it was only a matter of time before the Phoenix began in earnest to search for me. I didn't know what had taken them so long.

It made sense; they needed to create a climate of fear. Why go after the focal point straight away? They would have no way of creating the tension they needed in order to control the population.

Chapter Forty-One

Three months of the Phoenix's passed before the inevitable eventually happened.

The glass shattered with the chilling sound of impending danger.

I knew what it meant.

They had come for me.